KILLING HEMINGWAY

ARTHUR BYRNE

This is a work of fiction. The characters, events, and story contained within, are created within the fertile imagination of the author. Any resemblance to persons, whether living or dead, or any events, are purely coincidental with the single exception of Nobel physicist Dr. Wolfgang Ketterle who was used with his permission.

KILLING
HEMINGWAY

CHAPTER 1

"Mr. Chompers is the best tortoise who ever lived."
– Theodore Alexander

Theodore was six years old and lived in Seattle. He had been a first grader for fourteen days. After the first week, he said to his mom, "Mrs. Braunshausen hasn't been giving us any homework. You may need to talk to the principal about her."

Teddy had been looking forward to school since he was three. Kindergarten, which was only half days, had been a disappointment. He didn't understand why they wasted valuable time with naps. His mother explained that the break was for the teacher.

His satchel already had the three mechanical pencils, an eraser, a ruler, and a Uni-ball pen with a cap, loaded up. Teddy put the red spiral notebook and the yellow pad he used for drawing in the main part.

His mother had started to read to him before he was born. She used to be an executive for Simon & Schuster in New York, but now worked as a magazine editor.

That was where she met Teddy's father, who had spent eight years as the youngest hedge fund manager at Lehman Brothers. Teddy tells people, "They fell in love and moved to Seattle to have me because the air is cleaner."

"Teddy dear, your breakfast is going to get cold," his mother said through the bedroom door.

"Coming Mom."

They had a woman who cooked and cleaned, but Mrs. Alexander always made breakfast for him and his father. It was Teddy's third favorite part of the day.

This day, she made biscuits with eggs, Swiss cheese, and bacon.

"The biscuits are awesome, Mom."

"They really are, honey."

"I do like cooking for my boys."

"Do you know what today is?" Teddy asked, though he knew they did.

Mr. Alexander said, "Is it the day you win a Nobel Prize?"

"Oh, I think that's next week," his mom quipped. "Today, they're going to announce the nominees for the Pulitzer. I think his book about Mr. Chompers is on the short list."

Teddy giggled. "Nobody has seen my book, and it is mostly pictures."

His parents made a big deal out of shrugging.

"Today, it is my turn to feed Mr. Chompers! Did you get the strawberries?"

"Yes, I put them in your lunch box."

Teddy was the only student to have a physics lunch box with a description of the Higgs boson particle.

Mr. Alexander drove Teddy to school. He had started a small tech company after escaping from Wall Street, and though it wasn't on the way, dropping Teddy off at school was Mr. Alexander's number one favorite part of the day.

Being dropped off at school was Teddy's second favorite part of the day.

Teddy tolerated, though just barely, the practice writing that they did each morning. His classmates were not very good spellers. While the other kids worked on describing the dog the teacher put up on the board, Teddy was writing his thoughts about Mr. Chompers and how he seemed to be in an especially good mood today.

Mrs. Braunshausen looked at his giant-lined paper, where he had written, "The dog is sitting. He has a ball at his feet. He looks bored, much like the writer."

She did not appreciate his prose, but much as Mrs. Braunshausen wanted to, she couldn't fault his penmanship, it was flawless. Mrs. Braunshausen loved yelling at children for getting their letters wrong.

"So, Mr. Smarty Pants, why don't you go up to the board and write a new sentence about the dog."

Teddy wrote, "The dog has chewed on his ball, as dogs are wont to do."

Mrs. Braunshausen said, "I think you meant to write "Dogs want to chew on balls.""

"No, I did not."

"That will be all, Mr. Alexander," she said and pointed to his chair.

Teddy returned to his seat and took out his red notebook. They were going to start doing math. He loved math.

In the first three weeks, he hadn't incurred the wrath of Mrs. Braunshausen during math because she would hand out papers with problems and then for the next thirty minutes, read a book at her desk. It rarely took Teddy more than five minutes to finish his work.

Once done, he opened his red notebook, which had the problems his father had written for him the night before. His first problems was $2x + 3x = 20$.

Mark, who sat next to him, didn't talk to Teddy much, but after three weeks, he was curious. He whispered, "What do you do in that notebook every day?"

"They are math problems." Teddy showed him.

"Why are there letters?"

"It is like a math puzzle."

"A math puzzle?" he whispered back, and then looked up to see if Mrs. Braunshausen was listening. She wasn't.

"It's called algebra. You have to figure out what the x means. It's a secret and if I solve it, my dad gives me harder ones. It's fun. Let me show you."

Mark seemed interested.

"You see, the x next to the two means you need to take the secret number times the two and then do the same thing with the three."

"What do you mean times?"

"Multiplication, but we don't get to that until third grade."

"And you already know how to do it?"

"I like math, and so does my dad."

"So, what is the answer?"

"Remember that x can only be one number. So, if we have four twos, that equals eight and then four threes, that equals twelve. Right?"

Mark's eyes lit up, and he said, "Eight plus twelve equals twenty!"

Teddy did a half dozen more problems, and then it was time for recess. Mark went off and played tether ball with his friend while Teddy sat on the wall and watched. He didn't mind being left out, and his mind was on what came after recess. He would get to feed Mr. Chompers the juicy strawberries his mom packed. Teddy was sure Mr. Chompers would love them. Everybody loves strawberries.

Recess was almost over when April, a cute little red-haired girl, was pushed over by Tommy from the third grade. She skinned her knee and started crying. Tommy laughed and ran back in the building.

Teddy helped April up and said, "He's a jerk."

"I know. He's mean to everyone." She was still sobbing a little.

When they got inside, Mrs. Braunshausen was still reading her book. April, no longer crying, asked for the pass to the bathroom.

"What happened to you?"

"Tommy from the third grade pushed me down. I skinned my knee, but it isn't too bad."

"Come on, let's go get that cleaned up," said Mrs. Braunshausen as she took April's hand.

A few minutes later, they returned, and Mrs. Braunshausen said, "Quiet down, everyone. It is time to feed Mr. Chompers."

Teddy sat up straight.

"Theodore, do you think it would be okay if we let April have your turn? She has been through so much."

Teddy didn't say anything. It was his turn, and it didn't matter if Tommy had pushed April down in the playground. He folded his arms and didn't gather around as April gave him his food. It was the worst day of school, ever.

History was next and the last subject before lunch. Mrs. Braunshausen asked the class, "Who was the first president of the United States?"

A few students raised their hands. Teddy sat with his arms folded.

Mrs. Braunshausen said, "Teddy, do you know the answer?"

"Of course, it's too easy."

"Well then, why don't you tell the class?"

He glared at her and said, "George Washington; who was the seventh president?"

Mrs. Braunshausen had no idea and didn't like his tone.

"Buzz, time's up. Andrew Jackson. Who was his vice president...in his second term?"

Everyone laughed.

"Listen here, young man, you have been misbehaving all..."

"Buzz, it was Martin Van Buren. Who was the eighth president?"

The laughter was bordering on hysterics. Even April was giggling a little.

"I've had enough of your tone. You are heading straight down to the principal's office if you don't stop your back talking."

Everyone went quiet. Their teacher's face was so red it looked like it might explode.

"Buzz. That one was easy, it was Martin Van Buren. I tried to give you a clue, but..."

"Get down to the principals' office, now!"

CHAPTER 2

Principal Marcus Clemens was six feet four inches of towering disinterest. His office was typical, with photos of people he once knew, some framed articles of his glory days playing college basketball. He had been the "Round Mound of Rebound" before Barkley came along. He had three years until retirement. In fact, if someone asked him, he could have told them how many days.

He heard the commotion and recognized the shrill voice of Mrs. Braunshausen. Good God, what has got her riled up, today?

"Principal Clemens, I have a very naughty boy here who has been disrespectful and should be sent home."

Teddy looked pleased with himself, and Mr. Clemens was intrigued.

"Well, you know the rules. I'll need a letter to his parents before I can do anything. Do you have a letter?"

"I will! I marched Mr. Smarty Pants down here and intend to return and write the letter, now," She said and then whirled around and went back to the classroom.

Mr. Clemens stood aside, and Teddy strolled past and hopped into one of the chairs in front of his desk. His legs didn't reach the ground, so he swung them casually.

"So, Mr. Pants, or do you prefer I call you Smarty?"

"That was a good one. Most people call me Teddy, Principal Clemens."

"Okay, Teddy it is, then. So, how did you put a bee in her bonnet?"

"That sounds like one of those 'famous old sayings' my father uses, but I don't know what you mean."

Mr. Clemens smiled and said, "It just means, what did you do to get her so angry with you?"

"Well, it is a long story, but we have this tortoise, Mr. Chompers. Perhaps you've heard of him?"

"Yes, I know Mr. Chompers. He's been the first-grade tortoise for over a decade."

"He has? I didn't know that. He's an excellent tortoise."

"A fine upstanding member of the Testudinidae community."

Teddy wrinkled up his face and asked, "Is that another word for tortoise?"

"It is the scientific name. So, continue with telling me about what happened."

"On the first day of class, we all picked numbers out of a fish bowl. I got fifteen. It means that I get to feed Mr. Chompers on the fifteenth day of school. That's today. I talk to him every day, and he always comes to the edge when I do. He likes me best."

"What happened?"

"Well, April got pushed down by that bully in third grade."

"Which bully is that?"

Teddy thought for a while and said, "I'm not sure I should rat him out."

"Whom do you like better, the bully or April?"

"April is really nice. She wears bows in her hair, is never mean to anyone, and shared her cupcake with me yesterday. His name is Tommy."

Mr. Clemens leaned back and said, "He has been in here more often than I'd like. I'll look into it. Now, what happened next?"

"Mrs. Braunshausen gave my turn to April. April is great and all, but it was my turn. I wasn't very nice to Mrs. Braunshausen after that."

"What did you do?"

"She asked me who the first president of the United States was, and I asked her who the seventh one was. It made her really mad, but I sort of kept making her look stupid. But it WAS my turn, and I told him, yesterday, that I was bringing him a special treat. Now he will be wondering why he didn't get it." Teddy hung his head and gave a heavy sigh.

"He's a wise tortoise, I'm sure he saw the whole thing and understands. What was the special treat?"

"Two strawberries. You can't give tortoises too much citric acid... I looked it up on Google. They really like strawberries, though, and two is okay. I asked my mom, just to make sure. She said it was fine. They're in my lunch box."

"Everybody loves strawberries."

"So, what are you going to do with me now?"

"You've made a strong case for dismissal, but if I send you back, Mrs. Braunshausen will go nuts. You're not the first student she's sent my way. What do you say you hang out here with me until lunch?"

"Can I do some math problems?"

"Do you have some with you?"

"I bring extras from home."

Mr. Clemens laughed. "I've never heard of a student bringing extra math from home. I love it. Okay, you stay here, I've got to head down to the third grade and have a talk with Ms. Pearson about Tommy."

"Don't tell him that I told," Teddy said, looking worried.

"Don't worry, I won't."

* * *

Teddy ate lunch with April. He knew it wasn't her fault she got pushed down. "How was Mr. Chompers today?"

She set down her peanut butter and jelly sandwich and said, "He was good, though I think he missed you. I know it was your turn, today. I'm sorry."

"It's okay. How's your knee?"

"It's fine. I've got a Little Mermaid Band-Aid."

"I remember that movie. I saw it last summer. You want a strawberry?"

April ate one, and Teddy had the other.

Tommy walked past and said, "You told on me to the principal!"

April looked scared. "I didn't tell Mr. Clemens. I didn't even see him."

"I'm not going to forget this," then he turned to Teddy, "Whatchya looking at, dork?"

Teddy stared at him and said nothing.

Tommy smacked the table and went to sit with his friends.

April said, "Why is he picking on me?"

"He probably has bad parents."

"Thanks for the strawberry. It was good."

Principal Clemens came up. "Hello, Teddy and April, how was lunch today?"

"I had peanut butter and jelly, and Teddy gave me a strawberry."

"That was nice of him. Teddy, when you're done, can you come back to my office? I want to show you something I think you'll like."

"Sure, Principal Clemens."

Mr. Clemens held up his hand for a high-five. "Player."

Teddy didn't know what he meant, but he gave him a high-five back.

* * *

Teddy knocked on the principal's door. "What did you want to show me?"

"Hey, Teddy. That was a smooth move with the strawberries. You like to do math problems, right?"

"Yes, I love them."

"Come with me."

They walked down the hall, turned left, and took another hall that went by the sixth-grade classroom and into the library. Teddy hadn't been to the library since the first day, when they were shown the school. "They have lots of books here. Almost as many as my mom's library.

"Your mom has a library?"

"Yes, she got a lot of books from her grandfather. He died, but it was before I was born, so I didn't know him."

Mr. Clemens opened a door to a room with two tables in it. At one of the tables, one of the older kids had a book and was looking frustrated. "How is it going, Jeff?"

"I'm trying, Principal Clemens."

"Good, you keep at it," he said and then turned to Teddy. "Could you wait here, there is someone I want you to meet."

"Okay," Teddy said and sat down.

After Principal Clemens left, Teddy said, "Hi, my name's Teddy."

"Hi, I'm Jeff."

"What are you doing?"

"I'm studying math, which I'm horrible at, but they said if I don't, I'll have to repeat sixth grade. My parents would kill me."

"What are you doing?"

"I'm trying to learn multiplication. Everyone else is good at it but me."

"Do you know your times tables?"

"I'm not sure. I don't think so. What's a times table?"

"Let me show you. It really helps. Math is like a puzzle, but if you know your times tables, it's like a decoder chart."

"A decoder chart?"

"Okay, get a new piece of paper."

Jeff said, "How old are you?"

"I'm six, but math is my specialty."

"Let's see what you've got."

"Okay, write one through nine down the side."

Jeff did it.

"Good, now write one through nine across the top."

"Okay, I can do that. What's next?"

"Do you know what a times sign means?"

"Yes, it's the x."

"Right, and what does it mean?"

"That's where I'm not sure."

"Do you like basketball?"

"I love it. I play with my older brother all the time."

"Okay, look at the two line down the side. Those are points. If you make one basket you get two points, right?"

"Yes."

"How many points do you get if you make two baskets?"

"Four."

"So if you've shot the ball two TIMES and they both went in, then two times two equals four."

"Yep."

"Write a four on the spot where the two line is under the two across the top."

"So if I make three baskets, then I have six points, do I put a six next to it?"

"Yes. Now, put in all the points you have through the nine."

Jeff wrote them down without any problems and said, "I can do three-pointers, too."

A man with a white shirt and glasses came in with Principal Clemens.

"Teddy, this is Mr. King. He's good at puzzles, too."

Teddy stood up, stuck out his hand, and said, "I'm pleased to meet you, Mr. King."

"Pleased to meet you, too."

"I'll leave you two," Said Principal Clemens. "When you're done, just send Teddy back to my office."

Mr. King took out a folder and said, "I have a bunch of puzzles here. Some are really easy, and others are harder. Do you like to race?"

"Like running?"

"No, like solving puzzles quickly."

"I'm up for anything."

Mr. King explained how it worked and told Teddy to fill in the little bubbles completely. He took out a stopwatch, and they began.

CHAPTER 3

"What happens now?" Teddy asked Principal Clemens.

"Before we get to that, what did you think about the puzzles?"

Teddy's eyes got big, and he almost leapt out of the chair. "They were so awesome! He had a bunch, too. I wasn't sure how many I was supposed to do because I figured you needed to talk to me."Mr. Clemens said, "How many did you do?"

"I'm not sure. I should have counted. I just know that when I looked up, it was almost time for school to be out. I told him I was in trouble and needed to get back to your office."

Mr. Clemens didn't want to laugh, but he couldn't help it. "I like an honest kid."

"I have good parents." He took a more somber tone and then asked, "I assume you have some bad news for me."

"Yes, Mrs. Braunshausen has written a letter to your parents. I'm afraid you're going to have to take it home and get their signatures. You'll need to bring it back to-morrow. Can you do that?"

"Sure, but what happens after that?"

"She'll probably say something condescending to you and then get back to, and I use this word in the loosest of possible terms, teaching."

"Will I get my turn to feed Mr. Chompers back?"

"Teddy, my boy, I honestly don't know."

"My friend in New York, Mr. Ternov, would call you a straight shooter. I like that." Teddy stood up and walked around the desk and stuck out his hand.

Mr. Clemens shook it. The bell rang.

Teddy took the long way so he wouldn't need to walk past his class room. His mother was waiting for him outside.

"How was your day, Teddy bear?"

Teddy didn't say anything as she pulled away.

"What's wrong?"

Teddy took a deep breath and said, "I have a letter from Mrs. Braunshausen."

"Oh?"

"I was disrespectful today."

"You were? That doesn't sound like you. What do your father and I always say?"

"I need to respect other people because it is the only way they will respect me."

"That is right, Teddy. Now, what happened?"

"It's a long story. Maybe we should wait until Dad gets home."

"Okay. Did Mr. Chompers like the strawberries?"

"That's part of the story," he said, folding his arms and looking out of the window.

* * *

The previous summer, the Alexanders had gone back to New York City to visit their friends. It was the first time Teddy had been on a plane, and he loved it. Seeing the buildings and sky scrapers made him wonder about everything. His parents were used to his inquisitive mind.

Mr. Garcia was a stock broker and lived with his wife in a nice building in Manhattan. Teddy learned that it wasn't called an apartment; they lived in the penthouse.

The second day they were in town, Teddy's mom and Mrs. Garcia went to lunch while his dad took a taxi into his old office. Mr. Garcia was the boss and could take the day off so he and Teddy could hang out together.

"Teddy, what would you like to do, today?"

"Mr. Garcia, I don't even know what my choices are."

"Do you like museums?"

"Yes! We have some in Seattle that are great."

"Do you like to play video games?"

Teddy tilted his head sideways and used an expression that could only be called "duh."

Mr. Garcia laughed. "Well, then I have a good plan for us. We will go to the Museum of Modern Art first. It is really big, but I think you'll like it. Then we can get some lunch. Have you ever had a New York City hotdog from a street vendor?"

"No, I haven't," Teddy said, smiling, "but something tells me I'd like it."

"Great, then after that, we can go to a secret place that I'm sure you will love. It is run by a friend of your father's and mine, Mr. Anatoly Ternov. He's Russian. Have you ever met anyone from Russia?"

"I don't think so, but I've met a lot of people, and I don't know if all of them told me where they were from."

"Well, today you will!"

Teddy learned that true New Yorkers call it MoMA. Teddy and his mother practiced writing letters every night, and he would work on them by spelling the names of her favorite authors. When he saw all the paintings, he wanted to write their names down, but he knew it would take too long. Teddy made Mr. Garcia promise that he would remember them so he could write them down later.

He pointed at the placard and said, "I'm pretty good at reading, but I don't know how to pronounce this word."

"That is Vincent van Gogh, it's called The Starry Night."

"Why does it say 1889?"

"That is the year it was painted."

Teddy gasped. He stood motionless and scrunched up his face as he considered the year. "That is over one hundred years ago. Has it been here the whole time?"

"No, he painted that before this museum even existed."

"When did MoMA open?"

"That is a good question, let's ask that lady in the blazer."

Teddy went up to a woman in a blue blazer and gray skirt and said, "Excuse me, when did your museum open?"

His cuteness was reflected in her smile, and she answered, "It opened on November 7, 1929."

Teddy turned to Mr. Garcia and said, "Can you remember November 7, 1929? I'll need to put that in my notes."

The woman in the blazer asked, "Are you writing a book, young man?"

Teddy said, "Not really. I'm five and three-quarters, but my mom and I are working on my reading and writing every day. I write a lot, but not enough for an entire book."

"You're a clever young man," she said. "Who is this gentleman with you?"

"He's Mr. Garcia. He lives in a penthouse and took the day off work just to hang out with me. He's cool."

The museum was a big hit with Teddy.

From there they went to the A & T Arcade. There were pinball machines, a jukebox, video games, two pool tables, and one that was called air hockey.

Mr. Garcia said, "I want to introduce you to someone."

From out of the back, a portly man with a neatly trimmed gray beard came forward and said, "It is my old friend, Mr. Garcia, welcome. You are here for game of pool, no?"

Mr. Garcia said, "I brought a friend in to meet you."

Anatoly Trenov came forward and looked down at Teddy and said, "Hello, little comrade, my name is Anatoly Trenov, what do they call you?"

Teddy said, "My name is Theodore Alexander, and I'm pleased to meet you Mr. Trenov." He reached out a hand.

Mr. Trenov shook it and said, "Do you like video games, Mr. Alexander?"

"Yes, I do," he said, looking at the air hockey table. "What's that?"

"That is best game in whole world. It is called air hockey, but you want to know what it should be called?"

"Yes."

"It should be called physics. Do you know physics?"

Mr. Garcia fished a couple of quarters out of his pocket and put them in the side of the machine. It started to whir.

"I don't know that word yet. What is physics?"

"It is what I did in Russia before I ran arcade."

"You're from Russia," Teddy said, sounding impressed.

"Da, do you know where Russia is?"

"My dad has a globe in his office. I could show you, but I don't know how to tell you."

"Is okay. Now, I tell you about physics. Do you know friction?"

"Nope, sorry."

Mr. Trenov pulled a disk from the air hockey machine and set it down on a table next to the machine. Come here. I want you to take one finger and gently push the puck across the table."

Teddy crawled up on the red leather chair and stuck his index finger out. He eased the puck across the table until he couldn't reach any farther.

"You see what happens when you stop pushing?"

23

"Yes, it stops."

"There is friction between the table and the puck. Now, let's go over to the air hockey."

Mr. Garcia put a chair next to the air hockey table and lifted Teddy so he could stand on it.

Mr. Trenov said, "Okay, I'm going to hold puck down, and I want you to push against it."

Teddy did.

"It didn't move, but now I'm going to let up and see what happens."

Teddy kept pushing, and when the Russian's hand came up off the puck, it floated across the table, hit the far side, and then bounced to the corner. It just kept going and going.

"Air hockey is like a frictionless surface. That is important in physics."

Teddy grabbed the puck as it floated past and gave it another, harder push and asked, "How do you spell physics?"

Mr. Trenov spelled it, and then Teddy looked at Mr. Garcia and said, "You got that? I think I can remember, but if I forget..."

"I got it."

"Tell me more about physics."

"I worked in the field of particle physics."

Teddy looked at Mr. Garcia, who said, "I've got it.

For the next hour, Teddy and Mr. Trenov played air hockey. Teddy was a nonstop question machine. Mr. Garcia did his best to take mental notes. When it was time to go, Mr. Trenov said, "I have enjoyed meeting you, Theodore. You are very bright boy, just like Mozart."

"Who's Mozart?"

"He was born Johannes Chrysostomus Wolfangus Theophilus Mozart a long time ago. He composed beautiful music when he was your age."

Teddy said, "Mr. Garcia, did you get that name?"

"We can look it up on Wikipedia."

Teddy shook Mr. Trenov's hand and said, "I'm glad we met. Thank you, Mr. Trenov."

Mr. Trenov shook his hand and said, "Come back anytime. I let you play for free."

When they got home, Teddy spent an hour writing down all they did that day. Mr. Garcia started making dinner while Teddy sat at the island and made him recall the facts he'd promised to memorize.

When Mrs. Garcia and Teddy's mom returned, he jumped down and gave her a hug.

Mrs. Alexander asked, "Did you have a fun time today?"

"Yes! I have it all written down. When dad gets home, I'll tell you what we did. It was so much fun," then he paused and looked at his mom. "Do you know about this Mozart guy?"

"Yes, I do."

"You never mentioned him. He's pretty cool."

That night at dinner, Teddy gave a lecture on physics and friction. Afterwards, Mrs. Garcia played some Mozart on the piano. Teddy was impressed and gave her a huge hug.

The next day, they bought Teddy a physics lunch box for school.

CHAPTER 4

Teddy didn't want his after-school snack. He went to his room. Usually he would unpack his satchel, but he just set it by the desk and sat down. He rested his chin on his arms and looked at the drawings he had done of Mr. Chompers.

A little shudder of almost tears came and went. Every time Teddy thought about what Mr. Chompers must have thought when he didn't get the surprise he had promised, it brought the shudder, but then he thought about Mrs. Braunshausen, and it was gone. She made him angry.

Teddy reached down and pulled out the letter. It was in an envelope, but the sticky part hadn't been used. He pulled it out and began to read. Teddy went from angry to disgusted.

It would be a couple of hours before his dad got home, so Teddy pulled up Dictionary.com and grabbed a book. Reading seemed to make time disappear, and he didn't want to spend two hours waiting.

When he heard the familiar footsteps of his father, Teddy closed his book and minimized the browser. He grabbed the letter and went downstairs.

His parents were talking in hushed tones at the base of the stairs. "Dad...Mom, we need to talk," he said and walked down the hall, turned, and went into the library. He crawled up on the barstool and said, "I think I need a drink."

Mr. and Mrs. Alexander had, over the years, got good at hiding their smiles when he was being serious. This time, it was a real challenge. His father said, "Juice box?"

"Apple, and you better make it a double."

Teddy's mom pulled up the stool next to him and said, "I'll have what he's having."

Setting four juice boxes on the bar, Mr. Alexander said, "I understand there were some problems at school."

Teddy took out the letter and said, "If you ignore the spelling and grammar problems, the letter is accurate. I was disrespectful...with one s."

Teddy's mother took a sip of her drink box and looked away.

Mr. Alexander had a better poker face and said, "Yes, I see. What I don't see in the letter is the why."

Teddy took a long pull of the apple juice, until they could hear the sounds of empty. He pulled the straw out and stabbed it into the second box and said, "She was mad because I finished my writing so quickly. Then, I was a little bit...What's that word you use when you say something but you mean the opposite?"

Mrs. Alexander said, "Sarcastic?"

"I was sarcastic. She asked me who the first president was, because I was the only one who didn't raise my hand."

Mr. Alexander asked, "Why didn't you raise your hand? You know that one."

"I know them all, Dad, but I was mad."

"Why were you mad?"

Teddy gave a heavy sigh and then told the story of the playground and how he didn't get to feed Mr. Chompers. He finished with a sad, low, "I really wanted to feed him."

His mother put her arm around him. "I know you did, Teddy bear."

Teddy sat up straight and pushed his mother's arm off and said, "After she asked me about the first president, I asked her about the seventh...and then his vice president. I made her look stupid, and that was disrespectful...but it was my turn, and she gave it to April! I'm still angry."

Mr. Alexander took out a pen from his breast pocket and signed the letter. He put it back in the envelope and said, "Sometimes, we all get upset."

Mrs. Alexander said, "I appreciate you telling the truth, Theodore. Why don't you go wash your hands for dinner."

Teddy took the letter and went back to his room. He usually felt better after telling his parents what he had done, but not this time. He was still mad.

* * *

Monday morning, and Teddy didn't head straight into his classroom. He went to the principal's office and asked the secretary, "May I borrow your copier to make a copy for my records?" He held up the envelope with the letter.

"Sure, Teddy, help yourself. Just put it in the tray and hit the button with the green light."

"Thanks."

When he got to the classroom, Teddy went right over to Mr. Chompers and said, "Hey, buddy, how are you, today? I'm sorry you didn't get your treat Friday."

Mark came up and whispered, "That was really funny yesterday. Did they send you home after lunch?"

"No, I did some puzzles in the library for the rest of the day."

"I love doing puzzles. What was the picture?"

"They weren't that type, but they were fun, too."

The first bell rang, and everyone went to their seats. Teddy dropped the envelope on Mrs. Braunshausen's desk and gave her a glare.

She smiled, smugly, and pulled out the letter. Her face turned red. She ripped the letter into pieces, pointed to Teddy and said, "Come with me, Teddy!"

* * *

Mr. Clemens opened the folder and read the results. Most days he fielded calls, filled out reports, and hoped for death or his lottery numbers. Today, he didn't mind the job.

"Sir, Mrs. Braunshausen is here, with Teddy, again."

Mrs. Braunshausen barreled through the door and said, "This boy needs to be expelled. He's a rotten egg, and I won't have him stinking up my classroom!"

"Do come in."

"In all of my years of teaching, I have never had the misfortune of teaching such a little brat. I don't know what his problem is."

Teddy said, "I find Mrs. Braunshausen to be unqualified to educate first graders."

She yelled, "Do you hear that! I have never in all my life..."

Mr. Clemens said, "Teddy, why is Mrs. Braunshausen so upset?"

Teddy said, "I don't know, I didn't say anything, I just gave her the letter back, signed."

"Then I don't see the problem."

Mrs. Braunshausen said, "It is his whole attitude. He needs to be expelled immediately! I demand it."

Teddy stood and removed the copy from his satchel. He set it on the desk.

Mrs. Braunshausen turned a shade of red that looked like it might need medical attention.

Mr. Clemens opened the letter. In the top left corner was a large "F" with a circle around it. The document was entirely marked up with corrections. At the bottom it read, Too many spelling errors, poor use of punctuation, especially the comma, and problems with grammar, force me to fail this paper.

Mr. Clemens looked at Mrs. Braunshausen and said, "Teddy, could you wait outside for a bit while I discuss this with Mrs. Braunshausen."

"Yes, sir."

"Please close the door, and take a seat."

Before she could begin another rant, Mr. Clemens held up a finger and said, "It isn't your turn to talk. Let's begin with a question. Are you mad because he corrected your paper, or because you are dumber than a six-year-old?"

"I don't have to take this!"

"Yes, you do. My god, this is dreadful. You misspelled three words, used the singular form of the verb to be when, as Teddy correctly pointed out, you needed the plural. And your use of punctuation is an embarrassment."

"I was in a hurry and..."

"You sent this pathetic letter home to the parents of one of our students? What do you think they thought?" Mr. Clemens stood, and his voice rose as well, "His mother is a magazine editor! You better hope to God she doesn't complain. Don't you have any pride?"

"I need to get back to my classroom."

"One more thing...Who is the seventh president of the United States, keeping in mind that I plan on calling your union rep after you answer."

Mrs. Braunshausen stormed out of the room.

"Teddy, will you come back in here please?"

Teddy came in and sat back down. "I'm sorry, Principal Clemens, but she gets under my skin."

"She's been living under my skin since before you were born."

"Am I getting kicked out of school? I really like school, but I don't think she will teach me anything now."

"No, you are not. In fact, I think I have a better class for you. Do you mind being in a class with older kids?"

"No."

"Good, come with me."

CHAPTER 5

Holli Pearson stopped saying five foot two and a half, after she started teaching third graders. She loved being among her little people. It was Miss Pearson's second year as a teacher.

"Hello, Principal Clemens," she said and came to the doorway.

"I'd like to introduce you to someone. This is Theodore, and I'd like it if you could make space for him today."

"Good morning, Theodore, I'm Miss Pearson."

Teddy said, "It is nice to meet you, Miss Pearson. You can call me Teddy...everyone does."

"Teddy, why don't you go sit at that chair over there, behind the girl in the purple. Her name is Sally."

Teddy turned to Mr. Clemens and said, "Principal Clemens, thanks for this," then he gave a little sigh.

"What's wrong, Teddy?" Miss Pearson asked.

"Oh, it's just that I'll miss the class tortoise, Mr. Chompers."

"We have a rabbit named Beethoven."

"I'm sure he is a nice rabbit, but Mr. Chompers is the best tortoise in the world."

Mr. Clemens said, "Teddy, don't you worry, I've got an idea how you and Mr. Chompers can still hang out. I've got to make a call, but I'll get back to you, okay?"

"Really!?"

"I can't promise anything yet, but you come by after lunch, and I'll let you know. Deal?"

"Deal!" Teddy headed off to take his chair.

Miss Pearson asked, "How old is he?"

"I've pulled him from Mrs. Braunshausen's class."

"You skipped him over second grade?"

"Yes, I thought sending him to the sixth grade might be too much of a shock."

"So, we've got a smart little boy here, do we?"

"He almost makes me like kids," Mr. Clemens whispered.

"Stop that. You love kids."

"I love my pension, but this one is all right. I haven't talked to his parents yet, so I don't know what they'll think. I'll let you know."

"Okay."

Miss Pearson went over to Teddy and said, "Teddy, this is Sally Peterson. I'll get the books you'll need. I can do that at the first recess. Until then, maybe you could pull your chair around and read along with her."

Sally turned around in her seat, "Hi, Teddy. You can share with me."

"Thanks," he said, looking down.

"Class, I'd like to introduce you to Teddy."

Everyone looked at him, and he sort of shrank in his seat.

* * *

Mr. Clemens had his secretary call Mrs. Alexander. When she was on the line, he said, "Mrs. Alexander, how are you today?"

"I'm fine. Is Theodore having a bad day again?"

"I'd say Mrs. Braunshausen is having a bad day, but I'd rather think of it as the best day I've had in almost thirty years of being a principal."

"What did he do?"

"I assume you read the letter he sent home?"

"Yes, both my husband and I did."

"As an editor, what did you think?"

"There were a few problems."

"Teddy thought so, too."

"Oh no."

Mr. Clemens laughed and said, "He corrected it and gave her an F."

"I am so sorry."

"I'm the one who should be apologizing for putting your child's education in the hands of...well...someone so ill equipped to do her job. That's why I called. I'd like to move Teddy to a different class."

"Teddy does tend to speak his mind and talk more than he should sometimes."

"He can be a bit verbose," Mr. Clemens chuckled and added, "but that's what I like about your boy. What do you think about a new class for Teddy?"

"I'm sure you know what's best. I don't believe I know the other first-grade teachers. What are they like?"

"Mr. Adams is a fine teacher, but I was thinking he might be better served by Holli Peterson, third grade. She is in her second year and one of the brightest teachers I've ever met. She absolutely loves teaching and hasn't got bitter and worn down yet."

"The third grade; why did you move him up two grades?"

"Because I thought it might be too much of a trauma to put him in the sixth grade."

There was silence for a moment, and then she said, "That's very kind of you, but do you really think he can handle third grade?"

"I wasn't speaking in hyperbole just then. Yesterday, after the incident, I had Teddy talk with one of our guidance counselors, who wrote his master's thesis on spotting exceptional children. He had Teddy do some puzzles, and they talked for a long while. In his opinion, Teddy's aptitude for learning was off the charts. Bottom line, he really should be in the sixth grade, but I feel he'd be better served in Holli's class."

"Everyone thinks their child is a genius, but this is... well...I'm not sure how to react. Do you think he'll be able to fit in with the other kids?"

"He's a good kid. I think he'll do fine. He did have one concern, though."

"Yes?"

"He's rather fond of the first-grade tortoise."

"Mr. Chompers, yes, we know. He was really disappointed that he didn't get to feed him on Friday."

"I was wondering what you and your husband would think about letting Teddy have Mr. Chompers as a house guest on weekends. I'd set you up with everything you need."

"We would be thrilled to have Mr. Chompers on weekends. Teddy will be so excited. Thank you so much, Mr. Clemens."

"Good, it's settled then. I'll let Teddy know and put his mind at ease."

* * *

As they were getting ready to start history, Sally asked, "How old are you?"

"I'm six. How about you?"

"I'm eight and a half. You must be smart."

Teddy shrugged. "I like learning."

History class went well. Teddy followed along and even knew one answer. Sally got called on three times and raised her hand almost every time. After history, it was time for recess.

Teddy made his way over to the jungle gym, where April and Mark were talking.

"Hey, Teddy," April said, "What did you do to make Mrs. Braunshausen so mad?"

Mark asked, "You didn't come back. I figured she killed you."

"I bet she would have, if Principal Clemens hadn't been there."

"Are you coming back to class?" April asked.

"They moved me to the third grade."

Mark said, "Wow, that's cool. What's it like?"

"It's okay."

They didn't notice Tommy come up behind them. "Hey there, babies."

Mark said, "What do you want, Tommy?"

"I just came to see my new classmate. How you doing, baby Teddy?"

"Fine."

Tommy towered over Teddy and poked him in the chest, "You're in MY class now. You step out of line, Teddy boy, and I'll pound you and your little baby friends."

April looked like she was about to cry.

"Oh, look, the baby is going to cry."

A couple of Tommy's friends, who had come up behind him, laughed.

Teddy yelled, "Leave her alone. You're a bully."

Tommy pushed Teddy and walked away laughing.

Mark said, "He's such a jerk."

April said, "I don't like him at all."

Teddy just watched him walk away.

CHAPTER 6

Three weeks rolled by, and Teddy made a friend, Sally. Most of the other kids in the class were in two camps: they hated him because he was young and small, or they were jealous of him always knowing the answer.

Sally just thought he was nice. She usually knew the answers, too, so it didn't bother her at all. As for his age, she desperately wanted a little brother, and her parents had messed up and had another daughter. Her sister was two, but much less interesting than Teddy.

Teddy liked Sally, partly because she was smart, but mostly because she held the important distinction of being "tallest kid in class." It carried with it a certain gravitas that reduced the amount of harassing he received from Tommy. Not all of it, but enough that life was bearable.

Sally had one more important quality. Her sister, who was in the sixth grade, had a pet rat. On a scale of one to really cool, pet rats fell just below tortoises. Her rat's name was Scruffy. Sally's sister, Judy, brought Scruffy to their class for Sally's show and tell.

Judy liked Teddy, too, and said that she thought Scruffy liked Teddy almost as much as Sally. Tommy was afraid of Scruffy. Tommy saw Teddy's smile and made sure to heap some playground misery on Teddy when Sally wasn't around.

It was Monday, which meant Mr. Chompers was back at his "during the week" home, and Teddy's room seemed a little less awesome. He wanted to do some math problems, but he was caught up, and his dad wouldn't add more until after dinner. Playing with the Lego blocks was a good second choice (well, third) if you counted playing with Mr. Chompers.

Teddy liked to build massive secret lairs. The entrance, which only existed in his mind, was always the same. One had to get across the raging river to the base of the mountain. There was a giant boulder, and behind it, through some bushes, was a path that wound its way halfway up the mountain. Another large boulder, just off the path, hid the entrance to a massive cave. The roof of the cave was high enough that he could build an entire castle inside.

It was the castle that he liked to design and redesign. Today, he decided there should be a main gate and two rows of outer walls. The first one would be sufficient to repel an attacking hoard, if they could make it through the secret entrance, but the second one was a backup. It was taller and had guard towers spaced between the towers of the outer wall.

A lot of time had been spent worrying about lighting, until Teddy realized the mountain was actually above an ancient volcano. His fortress would have geothermal heat and electricity generation.

If the bad guys got through the secret door, he would immediately cut all the light. His archers in the towers all had night vision goggles. Teddy considered giving them guns, but the sound from their shooting would echo and be really loud. Plus, they could go pick up the arrows and use them again.

Inside the second row of walls were the castle keep and a small village. There was a market, which had things like chickens, eggs, tomatoes, fresh bread, lettuce, and Hot Pockets. Sally had a little house, next to April's. They each had secret passageways into the main keep.

Teddy hadn't built the keep yet, but knew it would have a dungeon, ten bedrooms, a main hall, and a giant library, plus a master suite in the tallest tower. The tallest tower was double walled. A secret staircase between the walls wound all the way down to the dungeon where another secret passageway led to the path of the elders. It went through the mountain and came out on the other side.

Teddy's mom yelled up the stairs, "Teddy, you have a call!"

There wasn't a phone in his room, but there was in the guest room across from his, so he went in there and picked up the receiver. "Hello?" he said, tentatively, as he didn't get too many calls.

"Hey, Teddy, it's Sally."

"Hi, Sally, what's up?"

"I was wondering if you wanted to come to my house after school tomorrow?"

"Sure, but I need to ask my mom, just a second," he said, putting his hand over the phone and yelling, "Mom, can I go over to Sally's after school tomorrow?"

His mother climbed the stairs and said, "Ask Sally if her mother would like me to drop the two of you off?"

"My mom wants to know if your mom wants her to drop us off?"

There was some yelling on Sally's end, and it was decided. Teddy asked, "Do you think Judy would mind if we played with Scruffy a little?"

"She won't mind at all."

"Cool, see you tomorrow," Teddy said and hung up after she had said goodbye. His mom said, "That will be fun."

"It will, and I'll get to see Scruffy again."

"Remind me, who is Scruffy?"

Teddy rolled his eyes and said, "Mom, don't you remember? Scruffy is her sister, Judy's, pet rat."

"Oh yes, how could I have forgotten?"

"It's hard to imagine. How many rats do we know?"

She rubbed his head and said, "Your father will be home a little early, tonight. He suggested we go get pizza. What do you think about that?"

"You know my position on pizza! I love it!"

Teddy didn't feel like playing with the Legos anymore, so he picked up his walls and other bits and put them away. He sat down and pulled the yellow legal pad out of his desk. At the top was written, "Stuff to Tell Mr. Trenov." He crossed out the first thing on the list, because he didn't think "Went to the dentist" was worthy of their phone time anymore.

There were three questions relating to physics and now, above them, it read "I have a friend, now." He would tell him all about whatever they did at her house. Teddy added in parenthesis (Scruffy).

They had last talked on the Thursday of his first week in third grade. Mr. Trenov was impressed about the promotion and showed an appropriate level of enthusiasm that Mr. Chompers would be living with the Alexanders on weekends. Mr. Trenov knew some neat tortoise facts, which didn't surprise Teddy because his Russian friend knew everything...just like his dad.

Teddy couldn't sit still. He wanted to run and slide down the hardwood floors, but it always made his mother worry. When she was out shopping, his dad and he would race and sliding was allowed, as long as they didn't tell Mom.

He found her in the laundry room and helped pair up the socks. As he matched one of his father's argyles with its mate, he retold the story about rat show and tell. He mentioned how excited he was to go to Sally's, at least as many times as he mentioned Scruffy. Teddy was careful to point out that he understood that he was Sally's guest, and that the rat was just an added bonus.

"Do you think she will want to dress up dolls or play house?"

"I don't know, Teddy bear, maybe. Little girls like that sort of thing."

"I can't say I'm into playing house, but it would probably be okay with Sally. She's nice."

When his dad got home, they headed out for pizza, and Teddy made sure he was up to date on all things rat. He brought his red notebook so his dad could add some problems while they waited for their food.

Teddy said, "Add some extras, because I'm running out before lunch."

The rest of the night all he talked about was Sally.

CHAPTER 7

Sally opened the door and said, "This is my room."

"You have a lot of dolls," Teddy said, a little worried about what was in store for his afternoon.

"I collect them because my mom really wants me to be a princess."

Teddy laughed and said, "Princess Sally."

"I know," she said, shaking her head. "It's crazy, but check this out." She opened her closet and took out a red-and-white striped uniform. "This is my soccer uniform."

"I didn't know you played soccer."

"We play in the spring. It's fun. I'm fast."

"That's cool. Your dollhouse is really impressive," he said, leaning in and looking at all the tiny furniture.

"Thanks, I used to play with it, but not so much anymore. Want to play teacher?"

"What's that?"

"I'm the teacher, and you're the student."

"We just came from school."

"Yes, but we can make up our own class."

"Okay, Miss Peterson, where do I sit?"

"Let me move my tea party stuff. I don't play tea party anymore either."

Sally went into her walk-in closet and closed the door.

Teddy grabbed a stuffed bear and duck from her bed and put them in the other chairs.

Sally emerged from the closet in a skirt and white top. She had her hair in a ponytail. She smiled when she saw the additional students and said, "Okay, class, you did a great job on your math homework, and so I think we will start something new."

Teddy raised his hand.

"Yes, Theodore?"

"What are we going to study?"

"Chess," she said and got down on her hands and knees to pull a box from below her bed. "Have any of you ever played chess before?"

Teddy said, "The bear and duck said 'no'. I haven't either."

"Excellent, I'll teach all of you."

"She opened the wooden box and said, "Theodore will be white, and I'll play black. Mr. Duck and Ike the bear can watch and take notes."

Teddy giggled.

"What?"

"I was imagining Mr. Duck with a pencil in his beak."

Sally giggled, too.

Mrs. Peterson knocked and said, "Would you two like a snack?"

Sally said, "Mom, can't you see we're in the middle of class?"

"I'm sorry. Would you like a snack during recess?"

Sally said, "Yes."

"Thanks, Mrs. Peterson."

After Sally's mom left, Teddy said, "I've wanted to learn chess since I was little."

"It's really fun. My neighbor, Mr. Wagner, taught me last summer. He gave me this board. The pieces are weighted. See," she said and wiggled the queen in the air by her head.

Teddy did the same. "I know we're only pretending to do school, but I think I'd like to take notes. Okay?"

Sally was thrilled. "You're a way better student than my dad. I think he is just humoring me."

"You're a great teacher. Almost as good as Miss Pearson.

"She's the best."

Teddy took his red notebook out of the satchel, and a pencil. "Okay, now, where do I put the queen?"

* * *

Mrs. Alexander was reviewing an article as Mr. Alexander read. Teddy came barreling in the front door and yelled, "Mom...Dad...where are you?"

Mrs. Alexander said, "We're in here."

Teddy ran into the library and said, "It was great at Sally's. She had dolls, but we didn't have to play with them. She taught me how to play chess. It is so cool. Then we had a snack and played some more before her mom brought me home."

Mrs. Alexander asked, "Did you get to see Scruffy?"

Teddy hit his forehead with his palm. "I was having so much fun, I forgot about Scruffy. That's okay, though, I don't think he was expecting me."

Mr. Alexander said, "Your mother and I used to play some chess, back when we first started dating."

"You did! Do you have a board?"

"You'd have to ask your mother."

"I think it's in the game closet."

Teddy flew out of the room and there was the sound of boxes being moved and rearranged. He yelled, "I found it." He came running into the room and said, "Can we play?"

"Did you put the other games back?" Mrs. Alexander asked.

Teddy ran back out of the room.

He returned, winded. "There, they're all back."

"Did you do it neatly?"

"Mom! It's a closet, it isn't supposed to be neat."

They set the board up and Mr. Alexander volunteered to go first. After five minutes Teddy said, "Dad! You're letting me win. I can tell. Stop it!"

"How can you tell?"

"Because you moved your knight to the outside. That's a dumb move. Sally said so, and you're not dumb."

"Okay."

"It's fine for me to lose, because that is how you learn."

"Did Sally tell you that, too?"

"Yes. She beat me, but said her neighbor...I don't remember his name...but he beats her all the time. Now, though, she is lasting longer."

The game continued and Teddy lost. Then his mother took a turn. He had to lecture her, too, about not playing her best. Teddy lost, again, but it took longer. He gave her a glare afterwards. "I'm not sure you tried your best."

"Oh Teddy, it's just a game."

"No, it makes you smarter! Now, you play, Dad!"

Mrs. Alexander got a gleam in her eye. She stood up, left. Teddy said, "Where are you going?"

"I'll be right back."

Mr. Alexander whispered, "Your mother is much better than I. She played on her college chess team. I don't win very often."

"It's okay to lose to a girl, Dad."

"Especially one as cute as your mom."

"Hey, no mushy stuff during chess time."

Mrs. Alexander returned and set the chess clock down. "Five minutes, dear?"

"Just for the record, your mother throws like a girl."

Mrs. Alexander moved a pawn and slapped the clock. The moves were fast, and their hands pounded the clock. Teddy was beside himself. He jumped around and cheered at each move.

Mrs. Alexander forked Mr. Alexander's rooks, and Teddy's father knocked over his king.

"Why did you do that, Dad?

"It's called resigning. Your mother has me beat."

"That was so cool. Can you explain the clock to me? What happens when you run out of time?"

Mrs. Alexander said, "You'd have to ask your father about that."

Mr. Alexander chuckled at the chess trash talking. "Yes, your mother never seems to run out. When I run out of time, on the other hand, the game is over. See the little red flag?"

"Yes," Teddy said.

"When that goes down, it is over."

"Sally didn't have a clock. This is so exciting."

"Would you like to read a book about chess?" Mrs. Alexander asked.

"Yes, please."

That night, Teddy fell asleep reading about chess.

CHAPTER 8

Teddy settled into a routine. Weekends were for Mr. Chompers and chess. Sally would come over, Dad would get cornered, or Mom, but it was always the same, "Let's play chess!"

During the week, he did math after school and called Mr. Ternov on Wednesdays. Teddy was thrilled to learn his Russian friend liked chess, too. They would talk for one hour after dinner, and then Mrs. Alexander would insist he get ready for bed. Sometimes, he read one of his books with a flashlight or imagined chess positions in his head, even though he was supposed to be sleeping.

The weeks between Thanksgiving break and Christmas were filled with preparation for the holiday pageant. Miss Pearson asked for suggestions from the class on what they would choose to perform. Though she enjoyed Teddy's reading of Act V, Scene 1 of Hamlet, she explained that it might be difficult to find a Horatio to match his prince of Denmark. Teddy found this to be a reasonable argument against. He was not thrilled with her choice.

Teddy was an adorable sheep in the show and even had some lines with the camel, played by Sally, but he didn't find his theater debut to be the tour de force he had hoped. The Alexanders and Petersons, though, loved it. Shortly after the performance, between the pizza and ice cream, Teddy announced his retirement from the stage. Sally said he was better at chess, anyway. Teddy thanked her, and they both enjoyed their banana splits.

Christmas break was a mixed bag for Teddy. He got lots of new Legos, but also put to bed the whole notion of Santa Claus, pointing out, quite correctly, the logistical problems with both the travel and varying chimney sizes. The "reindeer's don't fly" point was added as an afterthought. He had considered breaking it to his parents in '97, but decided to let them live with the fantasy for one more year. The look on his mother's face made him wish he had let her have '98, too.

The other downside was that the Petersons went to San Diego. He didn't get to see Sally for two weeks. It was awful. Mr. Chompers, though, did take up a lot of his time. Teddy even made sure his tortoise pal had a stocking, too. Teddy didn't tell Mr. Chompers the truth about Santa, though. Mr. Chompers loved his first Christmas with the Alexanders.

Teddy was playing with his Legos when Mrs. Alexander got the call. "Hello, Alexander residence."

"Tracy, this is Vivian Peterson."

"Hey there, how is San Diego?"

"It is warm, and they have this thing called sunshine. I don't know why Seattle doesn't have some flown in."

Tracy laughed. "I should have asked for sunshine from Santa. Oh wait, according to a well thought out argument by Teddy, he doesn't exist."

"Ouch, that must have hurt."

"It did, but I'll survive. My little skeptic is growing up."

"The reason I called was because I'm afraid I have some bad news, well good news, but..." She sighed.

"What is it?"

"I think Tom is going to take a job here in San Diego."

"Oh no, Teddy will be so sad."

"I know, Sally, too. We don't know for sure, but if it does happen, Sally and I will stay here until the school year is over and then come down. We haven't told her. Well, we don't know for sure, but it seems like they may make the offer soon. I just wanted to let you know."

"I appreciate it, Vivian. It does sound nice, though, all those sunny days. Let's get together for lunch after the kids go back to school. You can tell me all about it."

"Okay. I'll call you next week."

CHAPTER 9

Teddy was thrilled when school began. His little mind continued to soak up everything like a sponge. The music teacher tried to talk him into taking up an instrument, and though he enjoyed her class, Teddy told her his schedule was full.

The new art teacher arranged for an after-school meeting with Teddy and his parents. She raved on about his drawings and tried to get him to enroll in some special classes after school. She asked, "Teddy, would you like to be a great artist?"

"Do they give Nobel Prizes for art?"

"Well, no."

"Then I think I'll let someone else make the art."

Teddy told his parents on the ride home that she was nice, but crazy if she thought he was going to do something outside of the sciences.

His father had to buy him a second red spiral notebook. The first was given a place of honor on his bookshelf. The complexity of the algebra problems grew by the day.

With four weeks left in school in the year, Teddy got permission from Miss Pearson to have a meeting with her and Principal Clemens. It was scheduled for the last ten minutes of lunch in his office.

Mr. Clemens said, "Any chance of giving me a hint about his meeting, Holli?"

"Teddy wouldn't tell me."

Teddy came in and stood by the edge of the big desk. He pulled out a piece of paper and unfolded it then read, "Thank you for coming, today. First of all..." Teddy looked down at the paper and said, "I think I'm just going to wing it."

"We're all friends here, what's up, Teddy?"

"This has been the best year of my life. Thanks, Principal Clemens and Miss Pearson."

They both nodded at the compliment.

"Well, as you know, I'm well over six and a half. Seven is just around the corner, and it's time to think about my future. I was thinking about math class."

Miss Pearson said, "You are the best math student I've ever seen."

"Thanks. That is what I wanted to discuss. I enjoy math, and doing the exercises is fine, but those problems haven't been challenging since I was four." He took out his notebook and opened it to the last page and said, "This is the sort of stuff I've been working on."

Mr. Clemens said, "That's impressive stuff."

"I was wondering if I could use the math period for something else."

"What sort of something else?" asked Miss Pearson.

"Well, I was watching a program on television, and they were talking about the importance of reading. I love reading."

"You are an excellent reader"

"I am. I think I could be better, though. The only way to get REALLY good is to do it a lot. I was wondering if I could go to the library and do independent reading study."

Mr Clemens asked, "Why do you want to read in the library?"

"They have a lot of books to choose from. Also," and Teddy looked down, lowered his voice, and continued, "I don't want Tommy to make fun of me."

"Is he still giving you problems?"

"Nothing I can't handle, but...if you don't want me to...I can keep doing third-grade math."

"What do you think, Miss Pearson?"

"I think it's an excellent idea. Maybe you could write a short description of each book and turn it in for extra credit."

Teddy's eyes flew open. "That's a great idea. It would help my writing, too. I think this has been a very productive meeting."

"If you weren't so busy, I'd ask you to run for the school board. We could use your help on the first Tuesday every month."

Teddy giggled. "I'm too little for politics."

"You are too smart for politics. Well, you two better get back. I think our ten minutes is about up."

* * *

That night at dinner, Teddy told them all about his meeting. "So, for the next month, I'll get to have extra time to read. It's awesome."

"What are you going to read, first?"

Teddy said, "We have lots of books in our library, Mom, so I'll try to find something that I can't read here over the summer."

Mr. Alexander said, "That's a smart plan."

"Today, I looked at a couple of books. One was about a doctor who was really busy. He had a lot of patients in his office who needed to be seen. The other doctors were at the hospital, and he was short staffed. A patient came in, and she had a letter. She told him about the concerns her boss had about her health and told her to go to the doctor. She said she didn't feel sick, but that he was insistent. She went on and on about the symptoms her boss thought she had and then finally said, 'Here, you read it.' She handed him the paper, and it was blank!"

Mrs. Alexander asked, "What did he do?"

"I had spent most of the time looking through history books, books on science, and the section on the history of magic. When I pulled it off the shelf, I was almost out of time. I put it back and will probably check it out, tomorrow. I'll get back to you on what happens."

Mr. Alexander said, "It sounds like a thriller or mystery."

"Yes, I think it was, but I didn't remember to write down the author's name."

The rest of dinner, they talked about their favorite books.

CHAPTER 10

Teddy awoke and couldn't wait to get downstairs for breakfast. The day before, Principal Clemens had given him some good news. The first grade would be getting a new pet at the start of the next year. Mr. Chompers would be changing his name to Mr. Chompers Alexander.

"Mom, don't forget, we get out at two o'clock, and we need to hurry because Sally has a soccer game at three. This is going to be the best day EVER."

"I know, Teddy bear. You went over it last night three times."

"I'm going to miss Miss Pearson over the summer."

"Summer will go by, and before you know it you'll be back in school."

"We get our summer reading list today. I'm excited. Can we go to the library tomorrow?"

"Sure, but I have some things to do in the morning. We'll go after lunch."

Teddy gave her a thumbs-up and ate his breakfast.

The school day was filled with fun stuff. After lunch, Miss Pearson handed out the reading lists. She handed a stack of papers to the first student in each row and asked them to pass the lists back.

"Teddy, I have something for you," she said as he looked at the list.

"Oh bummer, I've already read most of these."

"That's why I made you a special list."

"You did!"

"I have one for you, too, Sally."

"Thanks, Miss Pearson," Sally said and then gave Teddy a high-five.

The rest of the class was less enthused about the list, but their spirits picked up when the box over the giant tray of cupcakes was lifted. They played some games, and even mean old Tommy was in good spirits.

Teddy and Sally enjoyed their cupcakes and then went down to Principal Clemens's office. They both thanked him for being a great principal, and Teddy gave him one of his drawings of Mr. Chompers with both his signature and a tiny tortoise foot print.

Teddy explained, "The footprint isn't real, though. I drew it, because I didn't want to get ink on his feet. He told me to tell you thanks, too."

"Teddy, my man, you've made this a good year," and he shook his hand. "You and Sally have a fun summer, and we can get together for some more learning in the fall, how does that sound?"

Sally said, "That sounds great!"

"You're one cool dude, Principal Clemens."

Teddy and Sally headed over to the first grade. He said goodbye to April and Mark, and then they picked up Mr. Chompers because it was time to go. They went back to their classroom and got their things. Teddy handed Mr. Chompers to Sally and gave Miss Pearson a big hug and said, "You are the best teacher in the whole school."

"You made teaching fun, Theodore."

Third grade was over.

* * *

The soccer game was fun. Mr. and Mrs. Peterson brought folding chairs for Teddy and his mom. They sat on the side, and Teddy kept one eye on the game and one on Mr. Chompers, who was doing some exploring. Sally's team won 3 - 1.

Teddy and his mom went home to pick up his dad and put Mr. Chompers in his tank before going to Big Dave's Pizza House. The Petersons were already there when they arrived.

After eating, Sally and Teddy went off to play a video game. When they got back, the mood had changed.

Mrs. Peterson said, "We have some news, but I'm afraid you may not like it."

"What is it, Mom?" Sally asked.

Mr. Peterson said, "That company that I've been doing the consulting for wants me to head up their San Diego division."

"Are you and Mom getting a divorce?"

Mrs. Peterson said, "No sweetie, nothing like that."

Mr. Peterson said, "The job is in San Diego..."

"Oh, you're moving to San Diego. When will I get to see you?"

"We are all moving to San Diego. We just need to find a new house," Mrs. Peterson said.

There was only a brief silence. Sally crossed her arms and announced, "I'm not moving to stupid old San Diego."

At first, Teddy was worried about Sally because she was mad. The anger quickly turned into tears, and Teddy didn't know what to do. Mrs. Peterson started crying. His parents looked sad. Everyone was upset.

It wasn't until the ride home that the truth of the matter set in. "Mom..."

"Yes, Teddy?"

"Is Sally going to come back in time for school?"

"No. She will be going to school near their new home."

Teddy didn't say anything. A tear rolled down his face and then another. He rubbed his eyes and said, "I don't want Sally to move. She's my only friend."

"You'll make new friends..."

"But not like Sally. She's smart, plays chess, and doesn't make me play tea party with her. She's perfect. What will I do?"

The question hung in the air. Teddy put his face in his hands.

When they got home, he ran from the car to his room. It was the worst day...ever.

CHAPTER 11

Over the years, Teddy had developed a fondness for routine. Fourth grade had been difficult without Sally around, but he had survived. The next year, he skipped ahead to sixth grade. It was more of a challenge. There was the added benefit of getting away from Tommy the Tormentor. Mr. Chompers had remained his best friend.

Now, at twelve, while kids like April and Mark were kings of the grade school, he was a mouse running along the walls of high school. Eleventh graders weren't mean to Teddy, they were worse: indifferent. The teachers loved his mental acumen, but always wore a face of pity as they talked with him. The poor little boy among giants.

Teddy no longer had a favorite part of the day. Each one was like the others. There was stuff to be learned and little time for play, not that anyone wanted to play with Teddy. He hadn't talked to Sally in over a year. She was fourteen and had a boyfriend. His name was Josh, and Teddy wanted to hate him, but he also wanted Sally to be happy. It was an unsolvable conundrum.

Beyond every daily torment, the loneliness, and indifference, there was one problem that haunted him constantly: girls. He didn't see it coming.

The summer between tenth and eleventh grade had been uneventful. The first day back at school, nothing seemed to have changed, except, well, the girls. They were everywhere, in cute skirts, with long hair and curves that he had never thought about before. Some of the girls in his class would hold hands with their boyfriends or sneak kisses by their lockers.

His locker was next to Karen Rogers's. She was short by high-school girls' standards, only five feet, which made her barely taller than Teddy, who was tall for a twelve-year-old. They were in the same homeroom, and Karen always said "Hi" and asked him how he was doing each morning.

It had taken him most of tenth grade to say more than fine and okay. When they were lab partners in biology during the spring semester, he was able to talk with her like he did other grown-ups. She got mostly Bs and with his help, an A in biology. Still, it wasn't like with Sally.

Now, one week into eleventh grade, Karen had made the varsity cheerleading squad. Her outfit made Teddy uncomfortable, and he was in a constant state of indecision about whether to look her in the eyes or stare at her feet. Everything in between made it hard to breath.

The first Friday, Teddy and his father went to the football game. Teddy had never cared much for sports, except soccer, but wanted to learn. They sat with the other parents. Mr. Alexander, who loved football, especially the Washington Huskies, explained the basics.

The game was fine, but Teddy really wanted to see Karen. The cheerleaders were in front of the student section. She was always the one they threw up in the air because she was tiny. They won the game 34 - 17, missing the last extra point. Teddy had learned enough about football, so he was prepared to say something intelligent Monday morning at the lockers.

* * *

Teddy still loved his talks with Mr. Ternov. Saturday afternoon, after daydreaming about Karen, Teddy gave him a call. "Hey, how's it going?"

"Good afternoon, my little West Coast comrade. I'm just fine. People still like to play games."

"True," Teddy said and then was at a loss.

"What is wrong? You don't have story for old Ternov? You always have story."

"I think I have a problem that could ruin my life."

"That sounds serious. Tell me about problem, and I help."

"I don't know when it happened, but all of a sudden I can't stop thinking about girls."

A hearty laugh rolled out of the phone. "Ah yes, you do have problem. Wonderful problem that will definitely ruin your life. What is your problem's name?"

"Karen."

"That is nice name. Is she clever like you?"

"No, she mostly gets Bs."

"But she is a cutie, no?"

"She's hot. I don't understand girls at all, plus, the whole age thing."

"Age is only a number. When I met Mrs. Trenov, she was five years younger than me."

"How old were you?"

"I was twenty-five, and she had just turned twenty."

Teddy gave a heavy sigh and said, "I'm twelve, and she's sixteen. I think four years is probably insurmountable at this age."

"Da, this might be true, but the great thing about age is it always changes."

"Thanks, but that doesn't do me any good now."

"I know. Still, life is long, and when you are billionaire with Nobel Prize, you'll get plenty of the women."

"What if I get killed by terrorists or aliens before that?"

"Then I say you unluckiest genius I know."

"You're not at all helpful, you know that?"

"I know physics. Not so much about women. Maybe you need different Russian friend."

"Nah, you're a great Russian friend. I'll keep you."

"I keep you, too."

"Thanks, Mr. Trenov. I think I'm going to go and wait for five or six years to go by."

Teddy was tired. The inescapable conclusion was too weighty to think about. He slept until dinner and then went to bed early.

* * *

Sunday afternoon, and Teddy sat on the floor. Mr. Chompers enjoyed floor time, and Teddy watched as he explored the area under the bed. His imagination searched for a reasonable scenario where a sixteen-year-old cheerleader would fall for a twelve-year-old nerd.

His first attempt revolved around a blockbuster movie about a really smart kid who gets the girl and all the other kids are jealous. It was so popular that star quarterbacks around the country found themselves cast aside for the smarties.

The second fantasy involved a group of terrorists who take over the school. Teddy, who hadn't taken chemistry, yet, but figured the invasion would happen after he had, would whip up a batch of knockout gas and capture one of the bad guys. He would take his guns and use cunning and guile to hunt the rest of the terrorists down. The last one, holding Karen, would get a shot off, wounding him, but not stopping Teddy from shooting him right between the eyes. Karen would tend to his wounds and fall hopelessly in love with him. Teddy wasn't sure how to shoot a gun, though.

There was another problem: neither scenario addressed the issue of tall. Girls like tall.

He was tall for his age, but that didn't really help him, now. Jason Colt was six foot two inches tall. And yes, he was the quarterback. That wasn't all, though, as he had a 3.89 GPA, had been recruited by a dozen top football programs, and was friendly. He even knew Teddy's name. They sat next to each other in advanced calculus.

They weren't buddies, but Teddy liked him well enough that his day dreaming forbade him from seeing Jason struck down by a meteorite. He realized something then: that Jason would be leaving at the end of the year. Maybe, he would dump Karen for a college girl, and she would be broken hearted.

The story line seemed believable, but then when he was imagining her coming to him for comfort, it all sort of unraveled. He would only be thirteen, and that was still too young.

Teddy realized he couldn't do anything about the time gap. The daydream about aliens taking him away and bringing him back four years older, was fun, but not the sort of things one could hang their hat on.

Mr. Chompers had climbed on top of a rather thick dictionary lying on the floor. It took him a while, but he persevered. Mr. Chompers was nothing if not patient and determined. Teddy decided he would be, too.

He would start small. Talking was the first hurdle. If he could pull off a real conversation then who knew what would be possible. Teddy laughed to himself. If he wasn't careful, she might be married, with kids and grandkids, before he pulled it off.

Even if it did take him a while to get good at talking to her, each day the age difference would become less of an issue. Teddy could always find comfort in math.

CHAPTER 12

Teddy had practiced his opening remarks. He would be clever and charming. Teddy stopped at the drinking fountain in the hallway outside his homeroom. For some reason, his throat was really dry.

In homeroom, he sat next to Vikram, who was also smart, but had only skipped one year in school. "Hey, Vikram."

"Hey, Teddy. How was your weekend?"

Teddy shrugged. "You?"

Vikram shrugged and went back to his book.

Karen came in and sat in her usual spot near the window. Teddy had considered sitting on that side of the room, but it seemed too obvious. She wore jeans and a pink top. Her hair looked nice, and he changed his plans. He would open with a remark about her hair.

The announcements consisted of a lame attempt at putting a positive spin on the lunch special, a mention of tryouts for the school play, and a call for volunteers to help the bake sale fund-raiser. Teddy stopped listening after "meatloaf."

Homeroom ended. Teddy made sure to get to his locker first, which wasn't hard, since he sat near the door. He got his books out for first period just as Karen started twisting the combination on her locker. "That was a great game, Friday. You did a nice job cheering." Damn, he thought, he was going to open with a comment about her hair.

"Thanks, Teddy, but I didn't see you there."

"My dad wanted to go to the game, so I sat with him. I really..."

Jason Colt wedged himself between them and said, "How's my girl?"

"Great, how's my quarterback?"

There was some kissing, which was worse than meatloaf, so Teddy went to class.

First period was English class. Mrs. Taylor loved books, maybe more than Teddy. She had auburn hair, liked to wear gray, and treated Teddy like everyone else. He liked that about her.

Mrs. Taylor said, "Okay, quiet down." She waited one beat and continued, "In a moment, I'll be handing out our first book of the semester, As I Lay Dying by William Faulkner. Have any of you read Faulkner before?"

Teddy raised his hand.

"Teddy, what have you read?"

"I read Light in August three summers ago."

There was another beat. Teddy assumed she was figuring out how old he would have been at the time. He got that a lot. "What did you think?"

"I couldn't really relate to Lena Grove, but I liked Joe Christmas. He was interesting. It was a good read, though, admittedly, it's one of my mother's favorite books, and she explained some of the stuff I might not have caught."

He could tell she liked his answer.

"Yes, there are many layers to his writing. When Light in August was published in 1933, I believe, it was to mixed reviews. Now, it's a classic."

Teddy looked down. He wasn't sure if he should correct her on the year. He decided to keep 1932 to himself.

"Teddy, you'll find As I Lay Dying to be quite a bit different to read. It is written in a style called stream of consciousness. Does anyone know what that means?"

Wendy, a girl Teddy didn't know at all, said, "I believe it's where the characters thoughts tell the story, something like that."

Mrs. Taylor said, "Very good, Wendy. Yes, the characters have multiple thoughts, the way we do in real life. I can tell, now, that Rick's thoughts are elsewhere."

Everyone laughed, except Rick, who didn't seem to notice.

"Richard Baker, are you with us today?"

"Um, sorry, I was...no, what was the question?"

"Do you know what we were discussing?"

"You started talking about the new book we're going to read."

"Yes, what were you thinking about?"

Rick shrugged and said, "I don't know, just spacing out."

Mrs. Taylor turned back to the class, "That is what I mean, sometimes we focus on one thing, other times, like when we're stressed, our minds can wander. I'm sure Richard will stay with us the rest of class."

"I'll try."

"Good, now open your books to the first page, keeping an eye open for stream of consciousness. Richard, will you read the first page for us, please?"

"Sure."

Teddy had already started and was on page four. This stream of consciousness had piqued his interest. While Rick read, he tuned everything out and blazed ahead.

Teddy stopped reading whenever Mrs. Taylor would make comments. The class ended before he had to read, which was probably good since he wasn't sure what page they were on.

He read during history, too. Mr. Olsen was old, balding, and spoke with less enthusiasm for history than a cat has for a bath. The word on Mr. Olsen was that he lifted the test questions directly from the text book, in order, and if one read the chapters it was hard not to get an A. Teddy liked history, but not the way it came out of Mr. Olsen's mouth, all dry and dead.

It wasn't something Teddy generally did, not paying attention in class, but he figured that Faulkner was a part of American literary history, so he was technically okay.

He didn't see Karen again until lunch, but that was from across the room. He sat with Vikram. They discussed the weather while Teddy watched Karen and her friends giggle and laugh. Vikram found Seattle to be colder than he would have liked. Teddy couldn't disagree but said, "Yeah, it rains a lot, too, but I like how it looks. It's scenic."

"Yes, it is. Hey, my father is getting me a new computer this weekend."

"Really, cool."

"Have you done any programming?"

"No, do you know how?"

"Not yet, but I want to learn. You want to come over and check it out?"

"Sure."

"I'll call you when it's ready to go."

Teddy gave him their phone number and headed off to physics. It was his favorite class, and he was always the first to arrive. The beginning of the textbook was all stuff Mr. Trenov had explained, but there was some great stuff in the back half. Also, Mr. Heit was awesome because unlike Mr. Olsen, he loved his job...and physics.

CHAPTER 13

Teddy read in the car on the way home. His mother tried to make a comment about the book, but he shushed her. "Don't tell me anything. We can discuss it when I'm done. Okay?"

"Okay, but you know how I love talking about books."

"I do, too, but this one is special. I've never read stream of consciousness, and it's more challenging than the other stuff."

"That's one of the reasons I like it."

"But you can't tell me what the stuff means because I want to try to figure it out."

"Okay...but it's killing your mother, you know that, don't you?"

"I do," he giggled, "and I'll tell dad it was my fault... and Mr. Faulkner's. I think he'll understand."

Mrs. Alexander always got such a charge out of Teddy. She drove and let him read.

Teddy kept reading even after he got home. He sat in his room until dinner. Books weren't allowed at the dinner table, so, using one of his custom-made book markers, he closed As I Lay Dying and went downstairs.

Mr. Alexander passed the chicken to Teddy and asked, "How was your day?"

"There was some good stuff and some 'eh' stuff," he said. The "eh" was in reference to his debacle of a conversation with Karen, but his parents didn't need to know about that.

"What was the good stuff?"

"We started reading a book by William Faulkner, As I Lay Dying, it's really good. Have you read it?"

"Yes, a long time ago, but I'm not sure I remember much."

"Teddy shushed me on the way home. We're not allowed to discuss it until he's done."

"Did you shush your mother?"

"I might have," he said, with a smile. "Oh, a guy I go to school with, Vikram, might ask me to come over to his house on Saturday."

"Oh?"

"He's getting a new computer."

"I thought that computers were just for goofing around?" his father asked.

"Yeah, they are, well, except for the stuff you do."

"Thanks. So, why the change of heart?"

Teddy chewed for a while, then took a drink of milk and said, "He skipped eighth grade, so he's younger than everyone else, too. His parents are from India, but I think he was born here because he doesn't have an accent. I haven't had a friend since Sally left. He's nice and doesn't treat me like I'm twelve. It's like we're colleagues in a strange world of averageness."

His mother gave him the glare. Teddy had, the year before, taken to making disparaging remarks about his classmates, and she didn't approve. All of tenth grade, he complained about how stupid everyone was, and they had gone round and round about it.

Despite the mountains of empirical evidence supporting his position, Teddy was happy and didn't want to have an argument. He said, "Sorry, Mom. A strange world of unrealized potential...and disinterest."

"That's not a substantial improvement, but I'll take it."

CHAPTER 14

Vikram Mehra worked on arranging his desk for his new computer. It was Friday night, and in the morning they were going to go to the store.

It was a long time coming. Everyone he knew, all of his cousins, every other honors student, had a computer years before he did. Vikram spent hours in the computer lab at school and taught himself what he could. His parents hadn't let him take a computer class.

Vikram begged for years and then finally made a proposal two years ago. If he got straight As then he could get it. It was rejected when his mother pointed out that he would be getting straight As regardless. Admittedly, he had never got a B.

His parents were proud of him, but all his cousins got As, too. He needed something more. Then it struck him. Vikram said he would take extra courses and do well enough to skip a grade. That got his mother's attention. None of her sister's children had ever skipped a grade. Mrs. Mehra said that if his father agreed, then it was a deal. In the Mehra household, Mr. Mehra didn't really get a vote.

Vikram's parents' marriage was arranged. They both had grown up in Mumbai. The story of how their marriage came to be was often told when the grandparents were visiting. It was not the true story.

At sixteen, she was compared to Parveen Babi, a stunning Indian actress. She knew there would be no shortage of boys being offered up for marriage. She also knew that her parents would make the decision without any input from their beloved daughter.

What they didn't know was that she had met a boy the year before. Keeping a secret in her neighborhood was a challenge not dissimilar to climbing Everest... while doing a handstand. It was unthinkable. The boy liked to fly kites in the park.

She and her sisters flew kites, too. Meeting him wouldn't be hard, but doing it in a way where her sisters wouldn't immediately start gossiping about him was. At that age, every boy was discussed at length. She had a plan.

It took but the flick of a wrist to cause her kite to be tangled with his. She said she was sorry, and as they knelt down to undo her "mistake," she said, "Here, don't show anyone. Meet me next Saturday." The boy had smiled, nodded, and slipped the note in his pocket with the grace of 007.

For three years, they had met in secret, never more than once every couple of months. It was hard, but she knew that it was the only way. When she turned eighteen and the meetings between families began, she enlisted the help of her beloved aunt to work the boy's family into the conversation.

The aunt, who adored her niece, never mentioned her role or how they had orchestrated the meeting. It had been a secret among the three of them for twenty years. Three years ago, she had told her daughter, Sata, who promised to not tell anyone. She told Vikram.

Vikram adored his sister. Sata was a sophomore at Washington University and was definitely her mother's daughter. It drove Mrs. Mehra nuts because Sata was the only one who was immune to her special brand of passive-aggressive dominance. He missed having her around, but she came home on weekends, sometimes.

He heard the front door open, and Sata's voice rang out, "Rejoice, the beloved daughter has returned."

Vikram bolted downstairs to meet her. He couldn't wait to show her where his new computer would live.

* * *

Sata gave her brother a hug and said, "How's the family genius?"

"Tomorrow, I get my computer. Come on, I want to show you something."

Mrs. Mehra came in from the dining room. "You missed dinner. Why didn't you call?"

"I had a seven o'clock class."

Mr. Mehra gave his daughter a hug. "How was the first week?"

"Great, Papa, all my classes are great. I don't have a single boring teacher."

"Come on!" Vikram said, tugging at his sister.

"Oh, stop pulling your sister, she just got home. Let her have a moment of peace and some dinner."

"It's okay."

Vikram ran up the stairs, and Sata followed. He closed the door behind her and began describing all the important facts: hard drive, processor speed, monitor size, and especially where it would sit. Then he lowered his voice and said, "Sata, I've invited a friend from school over to see it tomorrow."

"I'm sure he will be impressed."

"His name's Teddy and he's, well, not Indian."

"Good for you. Mother will be pleased. She's always bugging you to make friends."

"I know! It is such a pain. He's cool, though. The thing is, he's twelve."

"He's twelve and in high school?"

"He's a junior, just like me, but he skipped four grades."

Sata laughed and said, "Oh, now you're in trouble. I can hear mother now, 'Why can't you be like Teddy and stop wasting your time on computer nonsense?'"

"I hadn't thought of that."

"You know it's coming."

Mrs. Mehra's voice boomed up the stairs, "Sata, your dinner is hot, and it will get cold if you don't eat it."

Vikram whispered, "See, I'm a little worried about tomorrow. Mom will invite him for dinner. I'm not sure..."

"You think your friend may not be able to handle Indian food."

"Not the way she cooks it. Can you help?"

"Leave it to me, little Brother. Do they know you've invited Teddy over?"

"Yeah, I asked if it was okay."

Sata winked. She bounded down the stairs, loudly saying, "It smells awesome."

Mrs. Mehra was pouring a glass of water when Sata sat down. "Now, tell me all about this semester."

"Not much has happened the first week. I had one paper assigned in lit class."

"Have you started?"

"I got the assignment four hours ago, so, no, I've not."

"Did they teach you that snarky attitude at school?"

"No, I learned it through the study at home program."

"You are going to send me to an early grave."

"I hear Vikram has a new friend."

"Yes, a boy from his class. They are going to waste their time playing the video games on that new computer your father is buying him."

"You made the deal, if I recall. And he worked really hard to skip a grade."

"He is such a smart boy, but one can always do better. Don't you forget that."

"If I do, you'll remind me, I'm sure."

"Such a mouth."

"Are you going to have him over for dinner?"

"Who?"

"Teddy, Vikram's new friend."

"Of course, he is a guest in our house."

"What are you going to feed him?"

"What do you mean?"

"I mean, he's an American. He may not be able to handle your cooking."

"Oh, so now my cooking isn't good enough," she said, reaching for Sata's plate.

"You know that's not what I mean. You are a genius in the kitchen, but our food is a little spicy for someone that has never tried it."

"My food is good enough for you, it will be..."

"You have been bugging Vikram to make friends, and he does, and you can't be a little flexible."

Mrs. Mehra didn't answer. "I don't bug my children. I guide you to make the right decisions."

Sata got up and hugged her mother. "You know what's best."

"I will buy some hot dogs in the morning. Don't tell your aunts."

"I love you," she said.

"Your grandmother says you are my punishment for all I put her through."

"It is an important job," Sata said and kissed her mom on the cheek.

CHAPTER 15

Just after 1:00 Teddy got out of the car and ran up the steps to Vikram's house. The door opened, and Mrs. Mehra smiled and waved to Teddy's mom.

"You must be the very clever boy who has skipped so many grades."

Teddy shrugged and said, "I guess so. I like to learn faster than they wanted to teach."

Mr. Mehra held out his hand and said, "It is very nice to meet you Teddy."

Vikram could barely stand it.

"It is nice to meet you, too, Mr. Mehra. Thanks for letting me come over and see the new computer. It sounds like you picked out a good one."

Mrs. Mehra said, "You boys have fun. I'll bring up some snacks later. Would you like something to drink, Teddy?"

"Water, please."

"Are you sure, we have Pepsi and lemonade that I just squeezed."

Teddy said, "You make it from real lemons?! We have the powdered stuff. I'd love to try the real stuff. Thanks."

Mrs. Mehra smiled and left for the kitchen.

Vikram ran up the stairs, saying, "My room is this way, come on."

Teddy ran after him. Mr. Mehra followed, too.

They all stood around the computer, and Vikram said, "Okay, are you ready?"

"Ready."

"I didn't want to fire it up until you got here."

"Cool."

Vikram hit the button, and the fans began to whir. The screen came to life, the Windows logo appeared, and both boys stared at the screen like it was a tiny miracle.

They both had used computers at school, but somehow having a brand-new one with all the latest processors, memory, and video card made it even better.

Mr. Mehra said, "So, what do you think?"

Vikram hugged his dad and said, "I love it. Thanks."

"Okay, now remember what you promised. That game is a secret between you, Teddy, and me."

"Got it."

"That means you need to play it with the volume down low. If your mother finds out, I won't admit that I know you."

Vikram and Teddy both laughed.

Teddy said, "Top Secret, sir. We'll be careful."

Mr. Mehra picked up the box and read aloud, "Half-Life 2, is this a game about science?"

Vikram said, "Mostly, it is about killing monsters."

He handed the game back to his son and patted him on the back. "Have fun." He closed the bedroom door on the way out.

Vikram carefully opened up the packaging. He put in the first disk and began the install. The super-fast processor made quick work of getting the game ready. Teddy commented about the speed a couple of times. Vikram was proud of his new computer. Finally, it was installed.

Vikram turned off the game. "Mom's coming," he said as he opened a browser and quickly brought a science study forum.

Teddy nodded in approval.

Mrs. Mehra said, "Boys, I have your drinks, could you open the door?"

Teddy hopped up and opened the door. She handed him the two glasses, and Teddy said, "Thanks, it looks great."

"You are welcome, Teddy."

"Thanks, Mom."

They waited until they heard her footsteps get to the bottom of the steps before clicking on the Half-Life icon.

Half-Life 2 opened up, and both boys just stared for a moment. Electronic sounds from a distant future poured out of the speakers. Vikram moved the mouse pointer over New Game and clicked.

Teddy said, "This is not what I expected. It looks so real, like we're in Europe or someplace."

Vikram said, "I know. My mom thinks games are a waste of time."

Teddy said, "I sort of did, too, until about thirty seconds ago."

Vikram laughed and asked, "You don't have a computer?"

"My dad has a massive one, and he is always asking me if I want my own, but until now, I didn't. What do we do next?"

"I guess we click on Chapter 1 Point Insertion."

The loading bar crawled across the screen, and the logo appeared before a giant face started to talk to Vikram and Teddy. They both yelped with delight.

"Awesome!" Vikram said.

"Wow, it looks just like a real train."

The train stopped, and a voice over an intercom welcomed them to city seventeen. Vikram moved forward and walked out of the train car. Teddy was speechless. The lighting, the Chinese food cartons on the platform, and the video screen were beyond anything he had imagined for a video game.

"Should we continue or look around?" Vikram asked.

"Go through the turnstile."

A woman asked if they were the only ones on the train. "She's kind of cute," Vikram said.

"They really need to give the train station a good scrubbing."

Vikram laughed and said, "My mom would want to clean up, too. What if that was part of the game, you had to pick up the trash before you went on?"

Teddy thought this was one of the funniest things he had ever heard. "Yeah, how long do you think people would tidy up before they got tired of it? Oh, go over there," he said, pointing to the right side of the screen.

They walked past two guys and overheard them talking about the guy on the screen. Vikram clicked on the handset on the pay phone. It pulled completely off the phone, and Teddy laughed. "That's awesome."

When Vikram clicked again, the phone handset flew off and bounced under a bench. "The detail is incredible."

One of the guards in a strange mask told them to go up the stairs. Teddy asked, "What if we ignore him?"

"Good idea."

The men in masks didn't like it. They followed the man down the hall, and he banged on a door. In the room was a chair, with blood all over the floor. Both boys were delighted.

* * *

They took turns killing monsters. Teddy couldn't remember the last time he had had so much fun. As Vikram cleared out a section, Teddy watched and wondered why he always had to be so serious. He liked problem solving. That's all video games were, one more set of problems that could be mastered. He was hooked.

Mrs. Mehra called up the stairs, "Dinner is ready, boys."

Vikram yelled, "Coming, Mom!" Vikram paused and then saved their progress.

Teddy had never smelled food like this before. The table had black bowls with all sorts of things he'd never seen. There were two plates with hotdogs, and Vikram sat at one of them.

Mrs. Mehra said, "I've made you boys some hot dogs."

Vikram said, "Thanks, Mom."

Sata said, "No hot dogs for me?"

Mrs. Mehra signed, "If you want..."

Sata winked at Teddy, "I'm just teasing you, Ma," she said and gave her mother a kiss on the cheek as she sat down across from Teddy.

It was a lively meal. Sata would tell a story from school and then say something to push her mother's buttons. Mrs. Mehra had a few quick comments, too. It was all in good fun, and there was a lot of laughter. Teddy finished his hot dog.

"Would you like another one, Teddy?"

His eyes darted to the plate in front of Mrs. Mehra. "Um, sure."

"Would you like to try the dalimbya?"

"Yes, please. I've never had anything like that before."

She put some on his plate, and Teddy gave it a try. "Wow, this is awesome. What's it called again?"

Mrs. Mehra shot her daughter a triumphant smirk and said, "It is called dalimbya; it is a local dish from Mumbai, where I grew up."

Teddy said, "I'm not very good with geography from India. I know New Delhi is north, and Bangalore is to the south, but that is only because a girl in my sixth-grade class did a project on them. Her grandparents were from there. Where is Mumbai?"

Mr. Mehra said, "It is on the western coast on the Arabian Sea. About halfway between those two cities."

Teddy was fascinated and couldn't get enough of India.

Mrs. Mehra brought out some dry fruit kulfi, and they continued to share stories. Mostly, Teddy listened, but he did tell them how he came to have a tortoise named Mr. Chompers.

When dinner was over, Mr. Mehra and Vikram drove Teddy home. It had been a perfect day.

He bounced into the house. His parents were watching a movie. Mrs. Alexander asked, "Did you have fun?"

"It was incredible," Teddy said, and looked at his father, "You were right, Dad, computers are great. I'm sorry I didn't believe you."

"It's okay. What kind did he have?"

"I don't remember the parts, but it was the new processor. It was really fast, and we played this great game."

"What was the game?" Mr. Alexander asked.

"Half-Life 2."

"That's a good one."

"You know Half-Life 2?"

"Yes, I've got it on my computer downstairs."

"You play computer games?"

"Sure, even dads get to play games. I've been trying to tell that to you for years."

"I just thought it was a waste of time, but you know what?"

Mrs. Alexander said, "I think I'll leave you boys to talk about your computers. I'm going to go read a book."

"Okay, Mom, but you really should stay. Do you play computer games, too?"

"Nope, that's your father's thing. I have my books."

Teddy turned back to his father as Mrs. Alexander left. "Oh, you know what I figured out?"

"What is that?"

"Computer games are like puzzles."

"Yes, I suppose that's true."

"And you always say puzzles make you smarter."

"I do."

"So, I was wrong, they aren't a waste of time."

Mr. Alexander laughed. "Sometimes they can be, but even if they are, is that so bad?"

This made Teddy think for a while. "Well, I don't want to waste my time on something that is JUST fun."

"Why is that?"

A long pause followed.

"I haven't stumped you, have I?"

"Well, Dad, I want to go to a good school. So, I need to make sure I try my best, right."

"How many twelve-year-olds are in your class?"

"Just me."

"So, you're the only one who has skipped four grades?"

"Yes. Vikram has skipped one."

"How would you assess your progress, then?"

Teddy grinned. He knew his father had a point. "I suppose goofing off has its place, too."

"That's why your old dad has Half-Life 2 on his computer. Because sometimes it is fun to kill monsters. Want to go play?"

"Yes!"

They played until it was Teddy's bed time. He was impressed with how good his dad was at the game. He knew all sorts of tricks. Teddy said, "So, is that offer to get me a computer still open?"

"Yes, but I'll do you one better."

"What's better?"

"What do you say we build one, together?"

Teddy's eyes flew open. "And I get to help?"

"You can do most of the work. I'll show you how."

"When can we start?"

Mr. Alexander went to the closet and pulled out a bunch of boxes. "I was sort of hoping you'd say that. I picked up a motherboard, graphics card, RAM, and hard drives today. We'll need to go get a new monitor in the morning, but that is all we're missing."

Teddy was jumping up and down. "Let's start now."

"But it is your bed time."

"Oh come on, just a little bit. I won't be able to sleep anyway."

"Go ask your mother."

Teddy ran through the stacks of stuff and out the door. He didn't ask for special favors often, but when he did, he combined solid reasoning with unstoppable enthusiasm. It worked. They stayed up until midnight and got most of the way done. Mr. Alexander promised they would go to Best Buy in the morning to pick out a monitor. Teddy had finally hit the wall and agreed before he headed off to bed.

It was the best day ever.

CHAPTER 16

The three weeks that followed Teddy and his father buying the computer were a blur. Teddy didn't come out of his room much. He and Vikram both finished Half-Life 2 on the hardest level and became regulars on a forum that discussed such things.

There was the temptation to neglect his homework, but he got in a habit of doing it during lunch and immediately after school. He was content with getting just As and no longer felt compelled to obsess over packing as much into his brain as possible. At least, not packing non-computer stuff in there.

Both he and Vikram started to teach themselves visual basic and then C++. The hours they spent learning to write code was always showed off to their respective mothers, to put their minds at ease about the amount of time spent behind locked doors.

Thoughts of cheerleaders and football hadn't been so problematic. Teddy still hadn't managed a decent conversation, but he still said "Hi" at the lockers, and that was something.

It was Monday at lunch, and Vikram was late. "Where have you been?"

"I went to Mr. Wilcox's room."

"Who's that?"

"He's the computer science teacher. Check this out," Vikram said as he slid the orange piece of paper across the table.

"Computer science club. You want to join?"

"I want us both to join. What do you think?"

"It looks pretty nerdy."

"We're the definition of nerdy."

"I know," Teddy said with a sigh, "but I was hoping we could figure a way out of nerdom."

"Okay, then let's go out for the wrestling team."

That made Teddy laugh. "Do you think, 'tragic death' would look good on my college applications?"

"Not as good as computer science club, but it would definitely stand out. What do you say?"

"Why did you go to Mr. Wilcox's class?"

"He's the teacher that sponsors the club."

"What do they do in the club?"

"Mostly talk about programming and stuff...I'd guess. I didn't ask."

"I'm in."

"Cool. The first meeting is on Wednesday."

"I'll tell the wrestling coach we've decided to go a different direction."

Vikram laughed and asked, "Are you going to eat your cookie?"

Teddy broke it in two and said, "I'm going to eat half of it."

Vikram thanked his friend, and they both watched as the table with the cheerleaders got up to leave. From behind a book, Wendy said, "Dream on, boys."

Teddy said, "What?"

"You heard me."

Teddy saw that Vikram looked embarrassed. "What are you reading, Wendy?"

"A Farewell to Arms by Ernest Hemingway."

"Is that for class? Is it on the list?" Teddy was worried he had missed something. He knew that he'd been paying less attention in class.

"No, it's just reading."

Vikram asked, "Is it any good?"

"Not really. You guys are going to join the com-sci club?"

Teddy said, "Yeah, we're thinking about it."

"They don't have any girls in there."

Vikram said, "So, we're not girls."

She rolled her eyes and said, "I mean, you won't find any of those pom-pom girls in your little computer club."

Teddy asked, "How do you know there aren't any girls in the club?"

"I looked into it last year. It was mostly those goth guys, you know, the ones who hang around with Seth."

Teddy said, "Well, if you joined with us, there would be one...sort of."

"Nice one, kiddo, I didn't think you had it in you. You've got newb written all over you. I would wipe the floor with those com-sci guys."

Vikram said, "In what?"

"Halo, what else?"

Teddy said, "We've been playing Half-Life 2."

Wendy rolled her eyes and said, "Yeah, that's a good game, but serious gamers play Halo."

Vikram said, "You're a gamer."

"Yep...newb."

Teddy said, "Then it's settled, we'll all join together."

"I never said I was..."

Teddy played the chicken card and began to bock. It had always worked before, but he wasn't sure of its power in high school. It had been a long time since he had needed it. Actually, he had only used it once, on his mom, so it wasn't really a good test. She had, though, ridden the roller coaster. Both Teddy and his father fondly remembered her screams.

Wendy set her book down and stared at Teddy for a long time. His chicken noises faded. She said, "I guess someone needs to keep an eye on you two newbs. They'll eat you alive if I don't."

CHAPTER 17

Teddy and Vikram hovered between excited and nervous. Wendy was fearless and walked into Mr. Wilcox's computer lab, ready for the first sideways glance that came her way. She took a seat in the second row, Teddy sat next to her, and Vikram next to him.

Seth, six foot two inches of teen angst dressed in the all-black uniform that was the goth custom, sat on the table at the front of the room and chewed on a straw. "So," he said and looked at Wendy.

"Don't even start, Seth, I was there at the class picnic in sixth grade, I know what happened...it wasn't a spilled juice box, like you claimed."

Seth had to decide between a snarky retort or feint, and he went with, "Whatever, Wendy. I don't care about you, anyway, but it seems you've made some friends. I don't know who Apu is, but your tiny little friend must be Teddy."

Teddy said, "His name is Vikram, and you're..."

"Whatever! I'm surprised you didn't join last year. I expected to see you."

Teddy didn't quite understand why he would have been expected and didn't know how to answer. Fortunately, Mr. Wilcox arrived, and he didn't need to.

"Hello, and welcome to this year's computer science club. Most of you I know from my class, but I see a few new faces. Why don't you introduce yourselves?."

"I'm Wendy."

"Vikram."

"Teddy."

"Well, Wendy, Vikram, and Teddy, good to meet you. What made you decide to give our club a try?"

Vikram showed no signs of answering, though it had been his idea. Wendy looked like she had an answer, but that it might not be well received by an adult. Teddy said, "I just got a new computer. I've never given them much of a chance, but now I think I'd like to learn more than how to use them to play games."

Seth said, "You mean you just got your first computer? Newb."

His minions laughed.

Teddy considered making a comment about being smarter than Seth, which was true, but he wasn't smart enough to do it well, so he just said nothing.

Wendy said, "He'll be done with his master's degree by the time he's your age, Seth. And by the time you lose your virginity, he'll probably run the company you'll be wetting yourself to work at, so I'd back off...juice box boy."

Mr. Wilcox didn't like confrontation and was ill equipped to ease hostilities, so he passed out some copies of the club rules and said, "Now now, we are all friends here. Computer science club is about learning and helping each other."

The five or six kids who weren't part of Seth's entourage, but didn't really know Teddy (or Seth or Wendy either), seemed to be considering which side of the uncivil war they were going to side with.

"Okay, now everyone grab a computer."

The banter was replaced with keystrokes as Mr. Wilcox put up an example of a firewall with a fatal flaw. Seth and most of the others were quickly searching for back doors, Easter eggs, and known weaknesses, while Teddy, Vikram, and Wendy read the material he had handed out.

Mr. Wilcox sat down and said, "Most everyone was here last year, so this is probably not something you've run across before, but what we are trying to do is understand how innocent programming decisions can make a computer or company vulnerable."

Teddy asked, "So, you're teaching us how to fight hackers?"

"Yes, in one sense, but mostly I want you to understand why it is important to think about a piece of computer code from many different perspectives, not just what it is designed to do."

Wendy seemed less angry and more intrigued than before and asked, "Okay, what do we do first?"

"Well, have any of you written computer code before?"

"Teddy and I have been teaching ourselves visual basic," Vikram said.

Wendy said, "I've done a little and some HTML."

"Good, then you'll be fine." He began running them through some of the questions he always asked himself when trying to find a weakness. Mr. Wilcox brought up an easier example and had them try to find the back door, just by reading the code.

Wendy found it first, but didn't give away the secret. Teddy and Vikram both noticed the notes the programmer had left and figured it out less than a minute later. Seth and his minions solved the firewall problem and were loud and annoying for a short while, but then gathered around one corner and started talking in lowered voices as Seth pounded on the keyboard.

In the middle of the second example, Wendy, Teddy, and Vikram's screens all went blank at the same time, then a picture of a fat man's bottom appeared. Mr. Wilcox yelled, "Seth, cut it out."

The picture disappeared, but the laughter didn't.

CHAPTER 18

Teddy couldn't sleep. There was a little anger over Seth and his friends laughing at them, but that was a small thing. He figured that Vikram, Wendy, and he could come up with something cleverer. This thought led to the possibilities.

Solving those few problems, though they were basic and for beginners, got him thinking about all he didn't know. There was a world, buried deep within the ones and zeros, that only a few people truly understood. It was a fraternity that was open only to the brightest. He liked that idea.

For the last two years, since he turned ten, he had thought about little beyond getting done with high school and going to college. Teddy was 90 percent sure he wanted to study theoretical physics. There was so much in books that he had devoted most of his time to reading about the subject so he would be prepared when he got there and maybe have a leg up on what would be his older competition.

Now, it was as if dawn had broken on a strange new planet. He stood there in his mind, looking out upon a world he was sure was there to be conquered. The best part was he had Vikram and Wendy standing next to him.

After the first meeting of the club, they had gone to the mall. All agreed on three things: Nachos are awesome, Seth was a dick, and they wanted to learn enough to get back at him and rub the smug look off his face. Vikram pointed out that they were way behind on the learning curve, but Teddy saw it slightly differently. "Yes, but we are way ahead on the smarts curve." Wendy gave him a fist bump for that one.

Teddy lay in bed and then heard a beep. His clock read 1:12 a.m. It was Vikram sending him a message. It read, Are you up?

Teddy hesitated, because he wasn't supposed to get out of bed in the middle of the night. He eased into the desk chair and typed as quietly as he could, "Yes, I can't sleep."

"Me either. I keep thinking about today."

"I know, me, too."

"I really want to get Seth. Any ideas?"

"Nope, not yet."

There was another bing in the chat. "Hey guys, what's up?" said Gurl3741

Teddy typed, "Who is this?"

"Who do you think? Do you even know any other girls?"

Vikram wrote, "Hey, Wendy, how did you know we were talking?"

"I'm not as ignorant as Seth thinks. I've got a few tricks up my sleeves."

Teddy typed, "That's so cool, but I've got to go... parents."

Teddy hopped back into bed. He thought he had heard footsteps, but then they stopped. He must have been imagining things. He waited and listened. It was fun getting the chat message from his friends. It was like having a secret club.

The brief adrenaline rush left him, and finally, sleep came. Teddy made a quick mental list of things he wanted to know. Tops on that list: what had Wendy done to find out they were online. Tomorrow, he would set off on an exploration that would make Magellan proud.

* * *

It seemed like only ten minutes had passed when the alarm went off.

Teddy was exhausted at school the next day. He didn't raise his hand with quite his normal enthusiasm. History was unbearable, as he was positive he knew enough about the American Revolution to last him well into his seventies.

Second period was art with Mrs. Sanderson, and they talked about the importance of composition in drawing. This was something he had considered carefully when he was six drawing Mr. Chompers. He liked the class but not today.

Vikram found him between second and third periods and passed along a book. "I found this in the library. I'll need it back at lunch, but I knew that there wasn't any way I could sneak in any reading in old man Randolph's class. It's about C language."

"Thanks, I'll see you at lunch."

Teddy had started to read a few forums online before breakfast and had learned one thing. C was the language he needed to learn first. Fourth period was free study and then lunch. Teddy took the book to the cafeteria, which was mostly empty before lunch started, and dug in.

There were examples one could try, and it was killing him that he couldn't sneak into the computer lab and work on them as he read. The lab was full every period except sixth.

Wendy sat down and said, "Hey, I didn't know you had fourth free, too."

"Hey, Wendy. Check it out," he said holding up the cover.

"I read that book last year."

"You already know how to program in C?"

"I know some, but not like Seth."

"I was thinking about how we could get back at Seth."

"Me, too, but I don't have any good ideas."

"I know his online ID. I don't know if he knows mine, but it doesn't matter. I can create a new account and then pawn him and do a screen capture."

"What does pawn mean?"

"It means to beat or crush. Guys hate getting pawned by girls."

Teddy's eyes lit up. "I like it. Are you good enough to beat him? What game?"

"Oh, I'm good enough. I'm not sure. I haven't decided, but I bet we could also post a video on YouTube."

"What's YouTube?"

"You really are a newb, Teddy, but you're cool. It's this new site where people make their own videos and share them."

"How much does it cost?"

"It doesn't cost anything. It's the Internet, it's free."

Teddy wrote down YouTube in his notebook.

"May I ask you something?" Wendy said, sounding more tentative than he had ever heard."

"Sure."

"How did you manage to skip so many grades? I mean, I can see how Vikram skipped one, but four, that's amazing."

Teddy knew the answer. He had imagined people would ask him something like this, and he actually had expected it long before today. He had considered flippant answers, long-winded, literal responses, and just shrugging, but none of that was true. The problem with being honest is that no matter how he phrased it, the response he imagined would be the same. He hated pity.

He hated lying worse.

"The problem with the answer is it sounds sort of sad and pathetic."

"How can being really smart be pathetic?"

"My parents are great, and I have an old Russian friend in New York. He and I talk about physics."

"I'm not following."

"You see, the secret to my academic success is partly because I'm curious about things, but that isn't the main reason. It's because I've never had any friends."

The look in her eyes wasn't what he expected. It was less pity and more understanding.

She said, "Until now, I've never really had any friends either. There was a girl in sixth grade who was like me, but her family moved to Virginia. I guess it doesn't matter, since we both have friends now."

They talked about coding for a while, and then people started to fill up the cafeteria. Seth and his pack walked over.

"Hey, sorry about yesterday. We always give the newbs a hard time. No hard feelings," he said and stuck out his hand.

Teddy accepted it. Wendy didn't.

"Don't be such a..."

"A what," Wendy said, her eyes narrowing.

"Relax. This is John Chow, we call him Chen, Tye Nguyen, we call him Tye Guy, and Jeff...we call him... Jeff."

Wendy sneered and said, "Was that supposed to be clever?"

"That time of the month, Wen?"

Wendy got up and left just as Vikram arrived.

Seth said, "I was just telling Teddy and your bitchy friend that we were just kidding yesterday. We always give the new kids a hard time."

Vikram said, "Don't worry about it."

"Cool, we'll see you guys at the next meeting." They walked away. Chen and Jeff gave friendly nods.

Vikram waited until they were out of earshot and asked, "What was that about?"

"I don't know. Maybe Seth isn't as bad as we thought."

"Wendy doesn't seem to think so."

"Can you watch my stuff while I grab lunch?"

"Sure."

Teddy went through the line. It was pizza day. The cafeteria food was fair at best, but he liked the rectangular slices of pizza they got once per week. It was most of the kids' favorite. The ladies always seemed to give him one of the bigger pieces. It was the one advantage to being small. He figured they thought he needed it.

Vikram went through next. They spent the rest of lunch talking about programming and whether Seth was a good guy or not. It was decided that C was a cool language, but the jury was still out on Seth.

CHAPTER 19

A month had passed. The football team was still undefeated. Teddy, Vikram, and Wendy sat together in the student section and mostly ignored the games. For Teddy, it was as if they had fallen into a secret world that held vast mysteries he couldn't wait to uncover.

The wind was cold, and Vikram went to buy hot chocolate for them. Teddy and Wendy promised not to continue the discussion without him. Wendy changed the subject. "How did you do on the algebra test?"

"I did fine."

"I only missed the second-to-last question. I completely misread it."

"It was a tricky one."

"Did you miss any?"

Teddy paused; he considered lying but said, "No."

"Do you ever miss any?"

"Well, not really."

"Seriously?! When was the last time you got a math question wrong?"

"In school?"

"What do you mean? Of course, in school."

"Then no, I haven't missed any questions."

"Even last year? In Mr. Wester's class?"

"Math is my favorite, but I suppose I'll get something wrong eventually."

"Are you saying you haven't ever missed a math question?"

"I got a history question wrong in fifth grade," Teddy said, though he was lying. He liked being smart, but he didn't want to seem like he was bragging.

"What about in English?"

Teddy just shrugged.

"You're awesome," she said and gave him a fist bump.

They talked about her cat for a while. Its name was Professor Fluffy McMittens. The band had taken the field when Vikram returned with the drinks. Teddy liked cats, but not as much as he did Mr. Chompers. Vikram loved cats. Wendy promised to bring a picture to school on Monday.

The band was playing "Let it Be" by the Beatles, and Wendy said, "Hey, isn't that Seth?"

Vikram said, "Where?"

"In the section with all the trumpets."

"It is him!" Teddy yelled.

Vikram looked confused. "How did we not know that about him?"

Wendy said, "I can't believe it. I'm so giving him crap about it."

Teddy laughed. He liked Wendy's enthusiasm. He had to admit, though, he did like the song. His dad liked the Beatles.

The rest of the game was more exciting than the first half. Both the opponents on the field and the opposing mascot, a silly looking bear, seemed to be getting the upper hand. They scored twice in the third and added a field goal in the fourth. On the last drive, down by four, the Bears ran off a thirty-yard pass play that got them across midfield.

Teddy and Vikram got caught up in the excitement and forgot about computers and coding for a while. Wendy rolled her eyes on more than one occasion. When a tipped ball at the line of scrimmage was intercepted, securing the win, even Wendy was yelling.

When the final seconds ticked off the clock, most of the students stormed onto the field. Teddy, Vikram, and Wendy decided to pass and chose to head to the diner on 5th. Teddy had got permission to stay out until eleven. He was pretty excited, and it was great having a friend with a car, such that it was.

Wendy drove a beat-up 1976 blue Plymouth Duster. It ran well, didn't look great, but to Teddy and Vikram, it was a Rolls Royce. Wendy hadn't had her license for long, but had just been granted friend ride-along privileges by her parents. Fall Friday nights were now Teddy's favorite day of the week.

* * *

"Alexander residence," Mrs. Alexander said.

"Hello, how are you tonight?" asked Mrs. Mehra.

"Is something wrong?"

"Oh, no, it is just a little too quiet around the house tonight."

"I know. Our boys are growing up."

"I miss Vikram being home, but he has found a good friend in your Teddy. Such a bright boy."

"Vikram is a wonderful boy, too. I know Teddy has been much happier since they became friends. I worried about Teddy being so young when he got to high school. Last year was tough."

"We have good boys. I'm being a silly old woman wanting him to stay my little Vikram forever."

Mrs. Alexander laughed. "I know. I wish there was some way to slow them down, but if having our little boys working hard at school is our worst complaint, we should count ourselves lucky."

"Yes, yes, it does seem like I do search for a reason to complain. I'm such an old fool."

"It's nice to have someone to be an old fool with, though."

"I was thinking the same thing. Why don't we get together for lunch and discuss how horrible it is to have honor student children who don't get in trouble and are polite and kind?"

"It's a heavy burden, to be sure. How is tomorrow around noon?"

"Mrs. Alexander, I will see you then."

"Please, call me Tracy...or Teddy's mom."

Mrs. Vikram laughed and said, "That is what Vikram calls you. He said the other day, 'Teddy's mom makes the best cinnamon rolls I've ever tasted.' Then he tried to take it back, but I wouldn't let him and used the guilt to make him take out the garbage."

"I've heard quite a bit about your cooking as well. It seems Teddy has developed a taste for curry."

"I'll see you tomorrow. We can trade recipes."

"I look forward to it, Vikram's mom."

Mr. Alexander kissed his wife on the neck. "I gather that was Mrs. Mehra."

"You are so clever. We were wallowing in self-pity about our boys out having fun on a Friday night without us."

"I thought you were thrilled that Teddy had a couple of new friends."

"I am, but I miss Friday night popcorn and movie night."

"We could still make popcorn and watch a movie, just like we used to do."

"I remember popcorn and firing up a movie, but I don't recall ever watching it much."

"Exactly," he said and gave her a squeeze.

CHAPTER 20

Teddy liked to get up early, but seeing 6:30 a.m. through blurry eyes made him roll over. He never woke up before 8:00 a.m. on a Saturday and rarely any later than 8:05 a.m. His foggy brain considered what could have interrupted his sleep, but only for a moment.

The second time the crickets started chirping, he heard it and sat up. He sat up and looked around. The sound stopped. Mr. Chompers seemed disinterested. A minute passed. A bird chirped. Teddy's head snapped around and looked straight at his computer.

He hopped out of bed and moved the mouse. The screen came to life just as the computer made a sound like a seal. A chat box was open, and all it said was, Wakie...Wakie. Teddy moved his mouse over the chat window, and it vanished and popped up on the other side of the screen. The sound of a laughing baby mocked him.

Teddy's fingers danced across the keyboard. Fifteen seconds later, he slid the mouse up and to the left; the box stayed put. He typed, "Who is this?"

"Who do you think, newb?"

"Wendy?"

"You've got to be kidding. No."

"Seth."

"I have to admit, I thought it would take you longer to catch the chat box."

"What do you want?"

"You up for an adventure? I've got a little surprise for you if you can meet me at the Space Needle in thirty minutes."

"What sort of adventure?"

The computer started to make clucking noises.

Teddy turned down the volume. Vikram joined the chat, and Seth wrote, "Welcome to the party, Vikram. It took you a little longer than Teddy boy."

Vikram wrote, "It took me a while to figure out what is going on. Who is this?"

Teddy wrote, "It's Seth. He wants us to meet him at the Space Needle."

"Why?"

Seth wrote, "You'll have to show up to see. L8r."

Vikram wrote, "Teddy, you think it's a trick?"

"I don't know."

"Should we go?"

"It's pretty early, but I'm kind of curious."

"AFK."

Vikram had been using a lot of shorthand lately, and Teddy didn't know what AFK meant. He Googled it. (Away From Keyboard).

Vikram wrote, "I asked my mom if I could bike up there. She said okay, as long as I am back by 2:00."

"What's at 2:00?"

"My aunt's birthday party. You want to come?"

"Do I need to get her a present?"

"No. I didn't."

Teddy wrote, "AFK." He went and knocked on his parent's bedroom. His weary mother said he could go, too. "I'm in."

"L8R."

Teddy didn't know that one either, but he got it before he had to do a search and wrote back, "Later." He got dressed, put his notebook in his satchel, and grabbed a book in case he was early (and his Swiss Army knife). He couldn't think of a reason he would need it, but with Seth, it was best to be prepared.

The Needle was only ten blocks. He and Vikram went there all the time, but Teddy lived closer, so he knew he would beat him there. Just to be sure, he pedaled with a little extra gusto. He was sure Vikram would be racing too.

When he pulled up to the bike rack, Vikram said, "I beat you!"

"Wow, you must have flown."

"I knew you would be racing."

"I should have hustled more."

Vikram started to look around.

"We're early," Teddy said.

"What do you think he wants?"

"To make us look stupid?"

"Probably."

A 1997, barely still-blue Honda Accord pulled up, and the window inched down. It got stuck halfway. "Hey, hop in."

* * *

"Hey, Seth, where are we going?" Teddy asked.

"Just get in...it's a surprise."

Teddy opened the door. Vikram flipped the seat forward and climbed into the back, kicking his feet through a bevy of empty coffee cups and McDonald's bags. Teddy got in the front seat. The car reeked of smoke. Teddy pulled the door shut just as Seth started to pull away from the curb.

A high-pitched squealing sound came from somewhere under the hood. Seth slammed his foot down, and the rpms drowned out the alternator belt until he shifted into gear.

Teddy wasn't entirely comfortable with their decision to meet Seth.

Seth said, "Okay, I've been giving you guys a pretty hard time, but I have to admit, you learn quick."

"Quickly," Teddy corrected out of habit.

"Whatever, grammar boy, don't be a dick."

"Sorry."

"Anyway, I did some snooping around yesterday and found something I know you two will love."

Vikram, leaning between the seats, "What is it?"

"Do you know who Wolfgang Ketterle is?"

Teddy said, "Of course, he won the Benjamin Franklin Medal in 2000 and the next year the Nobel Prize for physics."

Vikram added, "In 1995, he used diluted gasses to achieve Bose-Einstein condensation."

Seth said, "I knew you physics geeks would know him."

Teddy asked, "Why?"

"I know where he is going to be in about fifteen minutes."

Vikram yelled, "No way! Where?"

Teddy asked, "Is he giving a lecture?"

"He's buying coffee."

The obvious question hung there for a little while, then Teddy asked, "How do you know that?"

"I hacked his schedule. He is in town for a few days, visiting a friend that used to work with him at MIT. On his planner, it had only two appointments for the day: at noon, he is meeting his friend, but right now he is on his way to buy a cup of Pikes Place Roast at Starbucks."

Seth, with a flourish, pulled his laptop from a bag between him and Teddy. He set it in Teddy's lap. "Open it up."

Teddy did, and sure enough, there was a screenshot of a calendar. "All it says is the time and Pikes Place Roast? How do you know..."

"Because there is only one place that sells that type. The original, first-ever Starbucks, which is just down the block." Seth pulled the car into a parking garage.

Teddy shut the computer. He didn't like looking at someone else's private stuff, especially not one of his ten favorite physicists of all time. Reason, logic, and guilt were all defeated by unbridled joy, though. "You think I can get his autograph?"

Vikram said, "That would be awesome. You think there will be a lot of people bugging him?"

Seth said, "He won the Nobel Prize, not the Super Bowl. Nobody will know who he is, so I'm sure you can say hello."

They walked past the fish market, and Teddy didn't even check to see if they were playing catch with the fish. He loved to watch the guys yell out an order and then one of them would throw the giant fish to another who caught it and wrapped it. Today, though, it wasn't so interesting.

The tourists were out in typical numbers. People with cameras, children, and bags filled with Seattle stuff seemed to be enjoying the unusually warm and sunny morning. There were a few people outside the Starbucks, which was, in its own right, a tourist attraction.

Teddy scanned the crowd and didn't see Dr. Ketterle. They got in line and waited. When it was their turn to order, Seth went first. Vikram was next and seemed confused.

Vikram said, "I've never had coffee before. My mother says it will stunt my growth."

Seth rolled his eyes and said, "One cup won't. Don't be a dork."

Vikram ordered a bottle of water. Seth wasn't impressed.

Teddy didn't want any coffee or water, but he didn't want to look weird to Dr. Ketterle, either. He ordered the same thing Seth had and decided he would just hold it and maybe take one sip.

As they waited for their order, Teddy saw Dr. Ketterle get in line. He whispered, "There he is," and elbowed Vikram who almost dropped his water.

Vikram said, "Let's go talk to him."

A lady handed Seth his coffee, and he said, "I'll be outside. I don't really get a hard-on over physics."

The woman behind the counter said, "Hey, this is yours, right?"

"Oh, yes, thank you," Teddy said and took his coffee. "Let's go."

They walked up and stopped right next to Dr. Ketterle, and neither one spoke. He was reading the paper and didn't look up. Vikram gave Teddy a look. Teddy gave the look right back.

Their idol had noticed them and said, "Hello."

Teddy said, "Are you Nobel physicist Dr. Wolfgang Ketterle?"

He smiled and cocked his head. "I've done some work in the field of physics, yes."

A few people heard Teddy's question and turned a little to look at him. The physicist seemed a little embarrassed.

Vikram stuck out his hand and said, "My name is Vikram Mehra, sir, it is a great honor to meet you."

This made the man chuckle. He shook Vikram's hand and then found Teddy's waiting, too. "So, you boys enjoy the sciences, do you?"

Teddy set his coffee down and flipped open his satchel. "Yes, may I get your autograph, please?"

More people were starting to check out the two boys fawning over the man waiting for coffee. Those that hadn't heard about his Nobel Prize seemed unable to place the face and had no idea what the fuss was about.

Vikram said, "Teddy, can I have a piece of paper, too?"

"Mr. Ketterle, could you sign one for me and Vikram, but on different pages?"

Wolfgang took the notebook and wrote his name, then flipped the page and did it again. He handed it back to Teddy.

Vikram said, "Don't tear mine out until we get home, so it doesn't wrinkle."

"You boys look pretty young, what grades are you in?"

They said in chorus, "Eleventh grade."

"Both of you?"

Vikram said, "Teddy skipped four years. I only skipped one."

Wolfgang was now at the front of the line and said, "I stop in every time I'm in town to get a grande Pikes Place Roast, so I'll have that, please."

The woman behind the counter rang up his order.

Teddy said, "I have a friend in New York City who used to be a physicist, but now he runs an arcade."

Wolfgang looked down and said, "You know Anatoly Ternov?"

Teddy's eyes got wide. "You know Mr. Ternov?"

"Of course, he's a great thinker. When I'm in New York, we get together for a game or two of chess, and I..." His voice trailed off. Then he said, "You're Teddy Alexander, his little friend from Seattle."

Vikram said, "He knows you!"

"Everybody who knows Anatoly knows of Teddy Alexander," he said, taking his coffee from the barista.

Teddy was speechless. He wanted to jump around and scream, but not in front of a Nobel Prize winner. "He told you about me?"

"He tells everyone about you."

Teddy and Vikram followed Wolfgang out of the coffee shop. Those that had been listening were now watching Teddy and whispering among themselves. One person took a picture as they went by.

Outside Seth waited. Teddy said, "This is my friend, Seth, he's into computers more than physics."

Wolfgang gave a polite nod to Seth and then turned back to Teddy and said, "Have you picked a college yet?"

"I've been looking at a bunch. It's hard to decide."

"I didn't realize you were already in the eleventh grade. I guess I thought I had a bit more time."

Teddy looked confused and asked, "Time for what?"

"We'd love to have you at MIT, and looking at Vikram, I'd like to see your transcripts as well."

Vikram said, "Really?!"

The professor handed each of them a card and said, "I really have to be going. I'd love to sit and talk all day with you two about physics and your futures, but I'm meeting a friend. Send me an email, and we can talk later."

Teddy and Vikram each took a card and held it like a delicate piece of fine china. They just stood outside the coffee shop and watched him walk away.

When he was out of earshot Seth said, "No fucking way. He knew you!"

Vikram said, "You should have seen it, it was awesome. All the people in the line were looking at him because he won a Nobel Prize, but when he said he knew who Teddy was, they all started looking at my man here!"

Teddy was still in shock. "He knows my friend in New York."

Seth said it again, "No fucking way."

118

He kept saying it all the way back to the car. Vikram could barely contain himself. He kept going on about how much his mom would freak. Teddy wanted to scream or jump around or something, but he couldn't decide which, so he just sat in the car and listened to Seth and Vikram going on about it over and over.

It was the best surprise ever.

* * *

After Seth had dropped them off, Vikram wanted to go tell his mom right away. Teddy decided he was going to pass on Vikram's aunt's birthday party. Vikram understood and waved as he began pedaling like he was in the Tour de France.

Teddy walked with his bike.

I know you, you're Teddy Alexander kept playing on a loop in his mind. He started to cough. His stomach churned. He stopped at the park a few blocks from his house. The bench offered a chance to slow down his mind. There was a bunny, so Teddy focused on it.

The rabbit cleaned its foot and then went back to nibbling on some grass. Teddy thought it looked like a Peter, but then that seemed too obvious. The rabbit came closer. It was definitely a Peter, cliché or not. Much as he loved the sciences, he thought dissecting small creatures was gross.

He stopped looking at the rabbit and stared off at the passing traffic. Why did he think about biology? There wasn't an answer. His little voice was just as stunned by their meeting with his seventh-favorite Nobel Prize winner. He was number one now.

The rabbit had been joined by a squirrel. It didn't look like they were friends, more acquaintances. A bird flew past. Somebody was honking a horn at the corner. It wasn't interesting enough to look up. Teddy shivered, though it was warm. His mind was back online.

MIT sat on the Charles River in Cambridge, Massachusetts. It was a great school. That was all Teddy knew about the place, except that his favorite Nobel Prize winner worked there and knew his name.

Teddy thought about how long it took to fly to New York City whenever they went for a visit. It was a long ways away. He could imagine himself taking classes, learning all sorts of wonderful things, and maybe even having his best friend, Vikram, there, too. He started to cry.

He missed his mom. She was only a few blocks away, but it seemed like thousands. He would go home and tell her what happened, and then it would only seem like a few minutes before he would be done with high school and off to college, then a master's degree, and a PhD. Other people would know his name, and it would be nice like meeting professor Ketterle, but he really just wanted to have a girlfriend.

He wiped his arm across his eyes. The bunny hopped away, and he was alone with the life he had yet to live flashing before his eyes. An old woman walking a tiny dog asked if he was okay. He said he was, and started to explain, but then stopped. "I'm fine, thanks."

She gave him a look that actually made him less sad. She continued with her walk, and he looked for the bunny again. It was near a bush. He couldn't see the squirrel. Teddy took a couple of deep breaths. Watching the Peter calmed his mind, and after a while, he climbed aboard his bike and regained the excitement of being known by a Nobel winner.

He told his parents. Afterward, he called Mr. Ternov. They talked for an hour, but only a little bit about physics, his future, or anything scary. Mostly, they talked about chess and the rabbit from the park. Mr. Ternov agreed that it was the right name to give the rabbit.

CHAPTER 21

Teddy sat at his computer, thinking. It had been a weird Monday at school. A few people, before classes had started, smiled and said "Hey." He wasn't even sure who they were. Wendy had walked right past him and looked away when he tried to talk to her.

She had been avoiding him for a few days. He tried to call her Saturday afternoon, to tell her about meeting Dr. Ketterle, but her mother said she wasn't able to come to the phone. He thought she might be sick and sent her an email. She never answered back.

Vikram remained enthused, to put it mildly, about Teddy being known by a Nobel winner. He told everyone who would listen, which, admittedly, wasn't too many people. Seth, however, had retold the story a half a dozen times. It seemed that he told it well because when lunch period arrived, the whole school was buzzing about their little genius.

Seth had sat with Teddy and Vikram at lunch. He didn't tease them anymore. Teddy didn't see Wendy, and Vikram had said she was avoiding him, too. Seth said she was a bitch and not to worry about it. The rest of the day, all he did was worry about her.

When he got home, Teddy gave Mr. Chompers some more food and changed his water. When he returned to his computer, he saw on his friends list that Wendy was online. He typed, "Hey, Wendy."

His stomach churned. A minute passed without an answer. Teddy hated the silence. Another minute passed.

The chat window said, "What?"

She was sort of gruff by nature, but the length of time it had taken her to type those five characters made it seem almost hostile. He didn't understand.

"Are you mad at me?"

Almost immediately Wendy responded, "Have you done something I should be mad about?"

"I don't think so."

"You don't? Maybe you aren't a genius after all."

Teddy didn't answer for a while. He had no idea what was going on. Despite his best efforts, he couldn't figure out what had happened. He wrote back, "I'm sorry."

"What are you sorry about?"

Teddy didn't know, but if she was mad and he had done something, he knew he should apologize. Now, he didn't know what to do. "I don't know, but you seem angry. Can't you just tell me what I did?"

"Why don't you ask your new best friend?"

"Vikram?"

There was another long pause. "No...NOT Vikram. He's just as stupid as you are."

"I don't have a new friend."

"Don't you?"

It was horrible. He had never been so confused in his life. Talking with Wendy wasn't like solving a physics or math problem because they had rules. She seemed to be mad at him for no reason, and now she wanted him to talk to a new friend.

"I don't like you being mad at me. I didn't mean to do whatever I did."

"I've got to go. L8tr."

Wendy went offline, and Teddy had no idea what she was talking about. He called Vikram and told him about the chat.

Vikram said, "She ignored me all day, too. I think she's pissed at us both."

"What did we do?"

"I don't know. Girls are confusing."

"Why can't she just say what's wrong?"

Vikram said, "If you ever piss me off, I'll tell you why."

"Thanks. Me, too."

"I've got to go, but don't worry about Wendy, she can't stay pissed forever."

"Are you sure?"

"No."

"See you tomorrow."

Teddy was about to sign off when he got chat message from Karen that said, "Hey, Teddy, what are you doing?"

Teddy couldn't believe it. He replied, "Nothing, just got off the phone with Vikram."

"That is so cool about you meeting the physics guy."

"Thanks."

"Everybody was talking about you. You're a celebrity."

Teddy wasn't sure what to say to that, so he tried to change the subject. "What are you up to?"

"I'm bored and saw you online. I'm trying to figure out what to write for the school paper."

"Everybody likes football stories," Teddy offered.

"I did that last week."

"What about a movie review?"

"I was thinking I might write a story about you and the professor."

"Really?"

"If you're okay with it."

"I guess so."

"Awesome! :-) I'll think of some interview questions, and we can talk at school. Okay?"

"Sure."

"You're the best, Teddy. See you tomorrow."

Teddy couldn't believe it. He didn't think about Wendy after that. When he went to bed, it was hard to get to sleep because while it was cool to have everyone being nice to him, that was nothing compared to chatting with Karen.

CHAPTER 22

Tuesday was much like Monday, except that Teddy didn't notice the greetings, as his mind was elsewhere. At his locker, he sorted things and tried to look busy until Karen showed up.

"Hey, Teddy," Karen said.

He wanted to look casual like the guys in the movies that always get the girl. He wasn't sure how they did it, though. Teddy made mental note to pay closer attention. "Hi, Karen, you look nice today."

"This is my interview-a-genius outfit," she said and spun around.

The charcoal pleated skirt flared out and showed off her knee socks that had tiny kittens on them. The cobalt-blue sweater looked soft. Karen pulled a piece of hair back behind her ear. Teddy said, "I've never been interviewed before."

"Oh it's easy. I've written a bunch of questions that I think our readers will want to know about. All you have to do is answer."

"I can do that."

left, and then he heard something. Teddy looked up, and Mr. Olsen was staring at him.

"Mr. Alexander, did you hear the question?"

"Sorry, yes, there were thirty-nine signatories of the Constitution, plus William Jackson, who was the secretary, and signed to authenticate the results."

"That's correct. I'm pleased that someone has read the chapter."

Teddy hadn't read the chapter, but had read a book about the Constitution for a book report in sixth grade.

Mr. Bunts asked, "This wasn't covered in the chapter, but does anyone know how many delegates there were to the Constitutional Convention?"

Four minutes left, and it seemed like time might actually stop. Nobody raised their hand. Teddy didn't want to answer, he just wanted to go to the library. Mr. Bunts turned to Teddy, with an expectant look on his face. "There were fifty-five delegates. I've always wondered why sixteen of them didn't want to sign."

It was a perfect answer, because Mr. Bunts had a lot to say on the subject. He started off, and midway through what, on any other day might have been an interesting story, the bell rang.

Teddy was the first one out of the door. He made his way down the hall, up the stairs, and into the library. Karen wasn't there yet, which made sense as he doubted she was in as much a hurry. Try to be cool, he thought.

Karen came through the doors and with a little wave, said, "Mr. Alexander, thanks for coming," and then she giggled. "I'm sorry, I thought I'd try to sound like a professional journalist. It doesn't quite work when the interview is with your locker buddy."

"I've never been interviewed before, but it sounded professional to me."

"Thanks," she said, beaming. "Let's go in the back, where we won't be bothered."

Teddy made an "after you" hand gesture he'd seen on TV. He was ready for the nervousness to end.

Karen headed through the stacks, and Teddy followed. Her pleated skirt swished, and his mind, which seemed to be not working at all, wondered how long it would take to iron. Karen set her books down on the table in the corner by the window.

Teddy took a seat.

Karen opened her binder and flipped to a red tab, clicked her pen, and said, "Okay, first question. 'You're quite a bit younger than most of your classmates, can you tell us how you got to eleventh grade so quickly?'"

Teddy hadn't known what sort of questions she would ask, and this one, though reasonable, wasn't what he expected. "When I was in first grade, the principal thought I could handle something more challenging, so he moved me into the third grade. I guess I really like learning because I thought it was fun to get harder homework. The teachers kept giving me harder stuff. Eventually, I skipped another grade, and then I went from eighth to tenth grade when I took some summer courses."

Karen wrote really fast. Teddy waited for her to catch up and ask the next question. When she finished, Karen said, "That is really awesome. I don't know too many kids who like their classes to be harder."

"What's your favorite class?"

"Creative writing. I took it last year."

"Is that what you want to do, be a writer or a journalist?"

"Yes! I would love to write a novel or maybe work for the New York Times."

"Do you write stories and stuff outside of class?"

"All the time. I have a journal that I write in everyday and a notebook where I write short stories."

"That's cool. That is sort of the way I feel about learning everything. Even when I'm not in school, I want to learn more."

"Do you keep a journal?"

"I do, but it's extra dorky," Teddy said, not even noticing that his nerves had calmed down. He was having a conversation with Karen, and it wasn't scary at all.

She laughed and said, "What do you mean?"

"When I was little, my dad would give me math problems every night. I kept them in a notebook. You write short stories, and I do math. Math is pretty dorky."

"I don't think it's dorky at all."

"Thanks. What are your stories about?"

"Well, I wrote this one about a girl on a boat in the Mediterranean, and...hey, who's interviewing whom here?"

Teddy was intoxicated by her. "I think you're way more interesting than me."

"Nobody knows me, but you are buddies with a Nobel Prize winner, I think you are much more interesting, which brings me to my next question. How did you meet Wolfgang Ketterle?"

Teddy didn't want to mention Seth's hacking so he said, "We just ran into him at Starbucks. I recognized him from pictures I'd seen online when he was interviewed after winning. Vikram and I asked if we could have his autograph."

"Did he give it to you?"

"Yes."

"What happened next?"

"It was weird, I told him about my friend in New York, Mr. Ternov, and it turns out he knows him. I thought it was cool, but it turns out my Mr. Ternov has told him about me."

Karen was getting it all down. She asked for more details, and Teddy did his best. When the bell finally rang, Karen hadn't got to even half of her questions. As she packed up, she asked, "Maybe we could continue online later? I could IM you after dinner, if you don't mind."

"Sure, that would be great."

As Teddy made his way to his next class, he didn't even notice Wendy as he walked past her locker.

* * *

Teddy didn't do much after school. Mostly, he just hung out with Mr. Chompers on his bed and let his thoughts hover in idle. There was plenty to think about, much to sort, and even the pages of code that might hold an interesting puzzle, but it just didn't seem to matter.

They had pork chops for dinner. His dad told a funny story about work, but at soon as he was done, Teddy slipped back into a state of disinterest. Teddy helped clear the table and then went back to his room. The computer waited with him for the IM message he was sure would come from Karen.

He imagined she would eat dinner and then be eager to continue their interview. He sure was. Teddy didn't know what time Karen's family ate dinner, but he didn't figure it could last much past eight o'clock. It was eight thirty, and still nothing.

Another half hour crept past, and then a message popped up. It was Vikram.

"Dude, I just got done chatting with Wendy."

"She's not pissed anymore?"

"Oh, she is still mad, but not at me. She said you completely ignored her in the hallway."

"No, I didn't. I didn't even see her."

"LOL. She said you walked right past her and pretended she wasn't even there."

"She's done that to me all day."

"Me, too, but now she's just mad at you."

"I never figured out why she was pissed off in the first place. Did she say?"

"Yes, she doesn't like Seth."

"So?"

"We went and hung out with Seth and met Dr. Ketterle."

"I don't see what the big deal is."

There was a pause and then Vikram typed, "Women."

"LOL."

"I've got to go, I just wanted to let you know about Wendy."

"Thanks."

Teddy closed the chat window. He didn't like hurting Wendy's feelings, but it seemed a stupid thing to be mad about. It shouldn't matter if Teddy hung out with Seth, it didn't have anything to do with Wendy. He liked Wendy better anyway. Maybe if I told her that, he thought.

Teddy started an email. He got stuck after "Dear Wendy" because everything he wrote sounded stupid. He tried to explain that she was one of his best friends and Seth wasn't even really a friend. It got long winded, and he deleted it. Next, he wrote that she was special and shouldn't be so insecure. When he reread that part, the voice inside of him made a strong case for deleting. Teddy wasn't sure why, but his gut told him that using the word insecure, though accurate, would make things worse. Possibly worse on a scale he couldn't even begin to comprehend.

The more he tried to figure out a way to fix it, the worse it got. An hour passed, and Teddy was drained. He crawled into bed, turned off the light, and lay there worrying about what he would say to Wendy at school. As he got nearer to slumber, his last question to himself was, I wonder why Karen...

The IM window popped open.

* * *

Teddy threw the covers off and quicker than the flash was at his keyboard reading the message from Karen.

"Are you still up?"

"Yes," he wrote and let his fingers pause as his brain tried to come up with something amusing. His brain let him down and the painful pause was filled by a reply.

"I'm sorry I didn't get on earlier, but Jason and I had this huge fight. He was such a jerk."

Teddy was glad she couldn't seem him smiling. "I'm sorry, what was it about?"

"I was at the mall with my sister, and we were coming out of Old Navy, and I saw him talking with Justine in the food court."

Teddy didn't know Justine. She was tall, on the basketball team, and everyone said she was going to be a model. He had never had a class with her.

"I was going to go up and say, 'Busted', but my sister stopped me."

Teddy wasn't sure what Jason was busted for, but it seemed talking was a high crime, though it seemed like more of a misdemeanor. "Maybe they just ran into each other, and he was being polite?"

"That's what my sister said, so we went over to the Orange Julius and stood in line to watch him."

"What did he do?"

"He was totally flirting with her. I was pissed."

This is way better than an interview, Teddy thought. "What did you do?"

"I got my drink and then just casually walked up to the table...totally calm. You should have seen the look on his face, he knew he was trouble. Justine was her typical fake self. AFK POS."

Teddy knew "Away From Keyboard" but wasn't sure what POS meant. Obviously, she was doing something, so he had time to Google it. Parents Over Shoulder, he read and grinned. Being up past his bed time, sitting in the dark, chatting with the prettiest girl in school about her personal life was awesome. He wasn't sure if he should write something back. He typed, "No Problem," then deleted it before hitting send and replaced it with "np" and hit enter.

With a ping she was back. "Sorry, my mom is such a pain. Anyway, I gave Justine a dirty look, and she scurried off to hit on someone else's boyfriend. She is such a skank."

"What did Jason say?"

"Oh he was all 'We're just friends' and 'We were just talking about Mr. Hernandez's music class,' but I knew he was lying. I told him, too."

"You called him a liar to his face?"

"Well, no, but I said 'whatever' with a total diva attitude. Same thing."

"What did he do?"

"He got pissed and said I didn't trust him."

"You weren't the one in the food court with Justine."

"Exactly! You so get me."

Teddy didn't get her at all. He didn't understand girls. He especially didn't get the problems of a cheerleader and her football star boyfriend, but he liked that she thought he did. Before he could stress out about what to say next, she continued on.

"You know what I told him?"

Obviously he didn't know, but rhetorical questions were easy on chat, and he wrote, "What?"

"I told him we were so totally over. Then I threw the necklace he gave me at him and stormed off."

"Wow."

"My sister said something to him, but I don't remember what it was. Jason called me after dinner, and we fought on the phone some more. That's why I didn't call."

"That's a good reason. I understand."

"You are so sweet. Maybe we can chat tomorrow? I should probably get to bed."

"Sure."

"Nite, Teddy, see you tomorrow. xoxo."

She signed off before Teddy had a chance to reply, which was great, because he would have probably said something stupid. It was the x's and o's that made it really bad. He knew they meant hugs and kisses, though he wasn't sure which was which. He didn't care.

Teddy crawled back into bed but got right back up. He copied and pasted their conversation from the chat window into a Word document and saved it as a new file.

It was sometime after three in the morning when he finally stopped thinking about Karen.

CHAPTER 23

Teddy's morning was precisely calculated on the ride to school. He knew that if he took the front hall he would arrive too early, so he went the long way around, past the library, and approached from the other direction. During his many hours of lying in bed not sleeping, he had concluded that it was likely he would appear too eager the next day. Karen had, he was sure, always dated cool guys, and they never seemed eager.

In truth, Teddy hadn't done much studying of cool guys, as it seemed a waste of time. He had, however, watched a lot of television with his father when he was younger. His dad loved the show Happy Days, and the Fonz certainly knew what it was to be cool. Teddy wished he had a leather jacket.

He adjusted his backpack so that he was only using one strap. He had always been a two strap guy, as it was much more comfortable. One strap seemed weird, almost unnatural, but those thoughts vanished when he saw Karen at the far end of the hall. She would arrive at the lockers about ten yards before he did.

He paced himself to widen the locker arrival gap, just to be safe. She wore a pink button-down shirt and jeans. Teddy's palms started to sweat a little. He wiped them on his pants, cruised into his locker, and said, "Hey, Karen, how you feeling?"

"Teddy, thanks so much for letting me dump all my crap on you last night. It really helped." She pulled her biology book out and a blue folder.

"You're welcome. I really didn't mind at..."

Seth swooped in, grabbed Teddy by the elbow, and said, "Hey, I need to talk to you."

Karen put her hands on her hips and said, "Excuse me? Interrupt much?"

Seth sneered and said, "Listen pom-pom, we've got some stuff to talk about, it's a bit over your head."

Karen punctuated her dirty look with a solid locker door closing.

Teddy said, "Don't be a jerk. What do you want?"

"Well?"

"Well what?"

"What did you think about the package I gave you?"

"What package?"

"The code!"

"Oh, yeah, I didn't really look at it much. The first few pages were interesting. I'm not sure I would have gone about it that way, but I'm sure it will make sense when I get to the end. What did you want me to do?"

The look Seth wore was a mixture of incredulous and duh, with just a dash of "Are you kidding me?"

"I've got to get to homeroom," Teddy said.

"Just find the holes...unless you think it's too hard."

Teddy matched Seth's look with a solid "whatever" face. It was the first time he had tried it. It seemed like the high school thing to do.

CHAPTER 24

Teddy almost got to talk with Karen at lunch, but Jason interrupted, and she left with him to have another fight. Their drama was the talk of the school.

He overheard someone say that Karen and Jason had got back together but had another fight between fifth and sixth periods and were broken up again.

After school, Teddy lingered at his locker and hoped to run into Karen. Seth showed up again and said, "So, genius, you had all day, what did you find?"

"I didn't find anything. I was busy."

Seth scoffed and said, "I knew it, the code's over your head. Forget it."

Teddy was tired of drama and didn't want anyone else mad at him. "I'll look at it now." He pulled the sheets out and began to flip through them. On the seventh page he stopped and flipped back two pages and then said, "Here, this won't work. The subroutine on page seven is the hole because of this..." he pointed at page five.

"Well done, Teddy boy. I knew you could do it."

"Thanks."

"Come with me."

"Where?"

"The computer lab. I want to show you another one...if you think you can handle it."

"I'll try."

The lab was empty. Seth picked a computer in the back and fired it up. His fingers rapped on the keys for a few minutes, and then he said, "Here, try this. I'll hit go, and then you need to crack the login and find the back door."

Teddy sat down and started to use some of the tricks he had learned. Seth stood behind him and mocked each failed attempt. After five minutes, Teddy was about to give up. He had tried everything he'd learned from the club, and he didn't have any other ideas.

Seth said, "Is that all you've got?"

Teddy didn't answer. He stared at the keyboard. Seth started to say something, but Teddy held up a hand and said, "Hold on, I'm thinking." He started to type and then hit the enter key with a triumphant "Ha!"

"Okay, now find the back door."

It took less than a minute, and Teddy had it.

"Not bad, newb. Here, let me show you something."

"I need to get home."

"Don't be a pussy. I'll give you a ride."

"Why are you such a jerk all the time?"

"You need to learn how to take a joke, Teddy. Just relax, you'll like this." Seth wrote some code and hit enter.

Teddy was impressed. "What just happened?"

"You'll want to take notes, my little padawan."

Teddy shrugged and got out his notebook.

The next hour filled Teddy's notebook with hacking tricks. At 4:00 p.m., Seth gave Teddy a ride home.

The first thing he did was turn on his computer and check for a message from Karen. The only message was from Vikram. It just said ping me back.

Teddy typed back, "I'm home, now. What's up?"

Vikram wrote back, "I talked to Wendy."

"Is she still mad at us?"

"I'm not sure, but I did say we didn't mean to hurt her feelings."

"What did she say?"

"She didn't really say anything. She changed the subject and asked me about our calculus assignment."

Gurl3741 entered the chat and asked, "Hey."

Teddy wrote, "Hey, Wendy.

Vikram asked, "What are you doing?"

"I'm going to The Landmark to see a movie. I'll be by to pick you up in ten minutes, Teddy, and then we'll swing over and get Vikram."

"What's playing?," Teddy asked.

"Who cares? Be ready when I get there. Bye."

Teddy asked his mom if he could go, and she said yes. He changed clothes, fed Mr. Chompers, and tried to figure out what had happened to make Wendy forgive him. It didn't make sense, but he wasn't going to do something stupid and ask her about it.

By the time he went to bed that night, his world was back to normal.

The next day, he learned that Karen and Jason had stopped fighting and were the most popular couple in school, again.

CHAPTER 25

The next week was relatively uneventful until Friday. The undefeated season came to an end with a loss to the Blue Mustangs, who had only won two games all year, but managed to return two punts for touchdowns. The final score was 14 – 10. Jason threw three interceptions.

Teddy didn't really care about the loss. He was happy that Vikram, Wendy, and he were all pals again. They sat together in computer science club and avoided Seth.

Saturday, they spent just hanging out until Teddy had to go home. Wendy dropped him off, and he waved as she and Vikram drove off. It was cold and wet as Teddy walked up to the front door, but he was in too good a mood to notice.

His mom and dad asked about his evening, and he gave a shrug. He was becoming a real high school student.

Teddy brushed his teeth as his computer booted up. When he got on, there was an IM from Seth. Check out this buried treasure I found in some code at the university. He sent a link.

Teddy clicked on the link and read the piece of code. The code didn't seem impressive. Teddy wrote back, "This doesn't look like treasure to me. It's not at all efficient."

"Haha, that's what buried treasure means. It's sarcasm...newb."

"Oh, I get it now."

"Are you ready for another test?"

"Sure."

"I'm going to time you."

"I'm ready."

A piece of code came over the IM, and in parenthesis it said, "Find the weakness".

Teddy spotted it immediately, and wrote, "Line 78."

Another, longer code came back. Teddy scrolled through the lines as fast as the computer would go. He found the problem on line 256, the next one was on line 280.

Seth wrote, "Okay, you got the easy ones. Time to get serious."

"Keep them coming."

He did, for three hours Seth threw every tricky bit of code he could find, and Teddy cut through them like a lightsaber through alien butter.

Finally, Teddy wrote, "This is fun, but I'm going to bed."

"L8r."

Teddy crawled into bed. His brain was tired and alive. He liked the challenge that the code presented and was more than a little proud of himself for finding all the problems. The more he learned about coding, the more it was like chess.

Computer code is black and white. There are rules, and the more one understands, the better one is able to make the computer do what one wants. Teddy liked learning new tricks.

He wasn't sure about Seth, but he had been learning a lot from him.

Sleep wasn't far off. Teddy replayed some of the more challenging issues he'd uncovered and was satisfied. His mind wanted to keep at it, but a deep yawn told a different tale. There was always tomorrow.

Just before the curtain closed and he drifted off, it was as if a line of code had written itself into his mind. If Seth was teaching him all that he knew, then he must have a reason. Teddy's brain tried to work out the logic, but it kept looping back on itself, and the error message he last saw before he went to sleep was "Error: Why?"

* * *

Teddy didn't sleep well at all. His dreams were disturbing. An angry weasel had started chasing him in the park. He had ducked into a forest to get away, but the weasel kept coming.

In the dream, he knew that there was safety in a cottage at the center of the forest. Teddy jumped over logs and bolted down the path. He came to a clearing and saw the cottage. The weasel was just behind him.

He made it to the door, but the cottage was locked. It had a computer keyboard on it, and he began to furiously type as the weasel, which was now a dozen weasels, rushed toward him.

There wasn't time, he couldn't get in, he was just about to be swarmed under by hundreds of weasels when he woke up. Teddy lay in bed, exhausted. The clock said 5:30 a.m., so he rolled over and went back to sleep.

Three hours later, his mom was calling him down for breakfast.

Teddy crawled out of bed and went to the kitchen.

"Good morning, Teddy bear, did you sleep well?"

"Not really. I had some weird dreams."

"Oh, I'm sorry to hear it. Do you want scrambled or fried eggs?"

"Fried, please."

"What are you going to do today?"

"I'm not sure, yet."

"Well, a good breakfast should help get you started."

It did help. After he ate, he hopped in the shower and was ready for the day. Teddy got dressed and got Mr. Chompers out for some floor time. The computer messenger pinged, and he looked up to see a message from Seth. "I've got someone I want you to meet."

Teddy wasn't in the mood for Seth or anymore of his adventures. He just let the message sit there.

"Are you there?"

Teddy didn't answer.

Seth pinged him again and said, "Dude, stop messing around. I know you're there."

Teddy wrote back, "I'm busy."

"Doing what?"

Teddy didn't want to say he was playing with Mr. Chompers so he said, "Studying."

"BS."

"I've got to go."

"Don't be such a pussy. Meet me in the same spot as last time in one hour."

Teddy was going to tell Seth no, but before he could, Seth was offline.

* * *

A popup box requested a private chat. It was from Vikram. Teddy clicked on the message and wrote, "Hi."

"You'll never believe what happened last night after we dropped you off."

"What happened?"

"You know that little park on John Street?"

"Denny Park?"

"Yeah, that's it. Well, after we took you home, we were just talking and driving around. Then she pulled into the parking lot at the park."

"Was there something going on at the park?"

"No, it was completely empty. We were just sitting there talking, and then she kissed me."

"No way."

"Yes. We totally made out for, like, three minutes."

"You're the man. Wendy's really cute."

"I know."

"How was it?"

"The kissing?"

"Yes."

"It was great. I even got to second base, sort of."

Teddy wasn't sure what each of the bases meant. "What do you mean sort of?"

"I got a little left boob action, but it was over her shirt. Does that count?"

"You felt her boob?"

"It was just for a second, and then a cop pulled into the parking lot."

"Wow, you really are the man."

"I really like boobs."

"Are you dating now?"

There was a long pause, and then Vikram wrote, "I'm not sure how that works. I mean, I didn't ask her to be my girlfriend, but she let me get to second base, so I think...maybe. How do I find out?"

"I don't know. Girls seem to have their own set of rules about everything."

"What if she was just using me for my sexy body?"

"LOL...you don't have a sexy body."

"Do you think I should start lifting weights?"

"No, I think she probably likes you as you are."

"Good, because working out would suck."

"LOL. Have you talked to Seth?"

"No, not since last week. Why?"

"It's nothing. I have to go. Congrats on 2B."

"Thanks. Talk to you later."

Teddy put Mr. Chompers back and slipped on his shoes. He wasn't sure what Seth wanted, but since he didn't have anything else to do, he decided to go meet him.

It was wet out, and so Teddy decided to walk. He had plenty of time to meet Seth. When he arrived, Seth was already there. Seth leaned across and opened the door and said, "You're late."

Teddy hopped in and pointed to the clock on the car radio and said, "I'm not late."

"I'm just messing with you. Lighten up."

"Where are we going?"

"You'll see."

They drove across Seattle to a part of town Teddy had never seen. It made him a little nervous. The industrial buildings had high fences and barbed wire. All the parking lots were empty, and nobody seemed to be around.

Seth turned down a street that looked like it headed toward the water. At the end of the street was a parking lot with a bunch of shipping containers.

Seth parked the car and got out. "You'll like Neal."

"Who's Neal?"

"He's a computer wizard. The stuff he can do is amazing. I've been telling him about you."

"Me?"

"Don't let it go to your head, but you're a natural hacker."

Teddy wasn't sure he wanted to be a hacker. He just wanted to learn to write computer code. Teddy thought hackers were mostly just jerks who messed up other people's hard work.

Seth walked around one stack of shipping containers, turned left between two other stacks. At the end was small shipping container with a door in it. Seth went through the door, and Teddy followed.

Inside the container were a desk and two chairs. Seth went to the wall on the right side and turned to smile at Teddy. "Check this out." He pushed the wall, and it spun open. It led to a group of four shipping containers stacked two by two with the interior walls taken out. It was a huge secret room.

In the center of the room was a ring of monitors and five computer keyboards. Two guys were playing a shooter game. In one corner was a ring of couches, and in the other was a ping-pong table.

Hanging from the ceiling was a hand-painted sign that read, Refugee Defense Camp: Anarchy

Teddy asked, "What does that sign mean?"

"You can ask Neal. He's over there. Come on, I'll introduce you."

Seth walked up to a guy who looked like he was in his twenties. He was tall with brown hair, and when he saw Seth said, "Seth, how's your kung fu?"

"Getting better every day. Here's the kid I was telling you about. Teddy, this is Neal."

Neal towered over Teddy, but not in a scary way. He held out his hand, and Teddy shook it. "I've heard you've got game."

Teddy just shrugged. He didn't really know what Neal was talking about. Teddy didn't know what to say so he asked, "What is this place?"

"It's my little hideout."

"What do you do here?"

"Sometimes, we mess around; other times, we party, but mostly, we dole out justice."

With that, Neal walked toward the ring of monitors. It was impressive, three rows of eight monitors stacked on top of each other arched in a semicircle around a curved table with five keyboards.

Some of the monitors had news feeds, two of them had stock charts, and others were just black with streaming code.

Teddy said, "It looks like The Matrix."

Neal smiled. "It's even better," he said and then tapped one of the guys playing a game and said, "Hey, give us a minute."

Both of the guys stopped playing and got up.

Neal sat down, "This is where we keep an eye on the world."

Teddy had to admit it was pretty cool. "What are you looking for?"

"Injustice, my young friend. Do you know what the number one danger to society is right now?"

"No."

"Corporate greed stealing the freedoms of the masses by gaming the system."

Teddy had no idea what he was talking about.

"They are draining the bank accounts of the population without anyone noticing. They chip away at the foundation until one day everything collapses and they are left running the world."

"What do you mean?"

Neal took out his wallet and pulled out an ATM card. "I never use this except for emergencies, but when I do, the banks steal a dollar. Do you think it costs them a dollar to process the transaction?"

"I have no idea. I've never thought about it."

"Trust me, it doesn't. The phone company tacks on charges, the credit card companies set up people to fail so they can add penalties, and even the utilities have extra fees that nobody understands. And it isn't just in the

U.S., the corporate overlords are the same all around the world."

Teddy wanted to ask what they do about it, but they were interrupted. A woman's laugh sailed across the room. Neal turned around and said, "What took you so long?"

"I said I would get your precious coffee after I finished running some errands. Look who I brought with me."

Teddy could see two women coming toward them. The one who had been talking and a redhead reached the computer pit, and they each gave Neal a kiss.

"Hey, Steph, how have you been?"

"I've got a surprise for you," she said and handed him a small box.

"Is this what I think it is?"

"Of course, have I ever let you down?"

"Never."

Teddy couldn't stop staring at the two women. The redhead looked like a super model, and the other one wore a sheer top, and he could see her black lace bra. Teddy thought she might be Japanese or maybe Korean. He wasn't sure, but she sure was pretty.

Neal said, "Let me introduce you to my new friend, this is Teddy. Jade and Stephanie here are a couple of computer ninjas."

"You're a cutie," Jade said and winked at the redhead.

Stephanie said, "I know, I could just eat him up."

Neal said, "We were just about to test his kung fu."

Neal sat down at one of the computers and started typing. Everyone gathered around. Teddy felt a hand on his shoulder. It was Jade. She was standing right behind him. He had no idea what was about to happen.

Neal said, "Okay, let's see you get past my firewall."

Teddy wasn't really listening to Neal, he was thinking about Jade. She was running her fingers through his hair, and he heard her say, "Come on, Teddy, you can do it."

Teddy snapped back into the moment and looked at his screen. He started to type, and people began to cheer. The first thing he tried was blocked. He isn't going to give me something easy or predictable, Teddy thought. He started searching and saw a weakness, but then he noticed a goto statement. It was a trick. He kept looking and thirty seconds later had an idea.

The noise of those watching faded. The hand on his shoulder was still there, but it didn't matter now. He was playing a game of chess against Neal and his code.

There were traps, code that looked like weakness but was just there to distract him, and then there was the tiny subroutine that looked meaningless.

The key was in how the computer reacted and if he could just slip in a command...

When Teddy hit enter, he was in a cone of focus that had blocked out everything but the screen in front of him. The screen flashed, and he had done it.

Everyone cheered. Teddy wasn't sure, but he thought Jade's boob had brushed against his shoulder.

Neal said, "I'm impressed. Nobody has ever cracked it in under two minutes. Most people can't get through at all, but most people aren't invited to the camp."

People were patting him on the shoulder. The red-head, Teddy had forgotten her name, gave him a high-five. A bunch of other guys patted him on the back. Seth said, "I knew you could do it."

"Did you do this, too?"

"Yeah, but it took me ten minutes."

Neal said, "Hang out here anytime you want."

Seth motioned for Teddy to follow him. Neal put his arm around Jade and Stephanie, and they headed off toward a door by his desk.

Seth said, "This place is great. If you like gaming, you'll love playing in the pit. There's never any lag. Oh, and check this out." He went up to a Pepsi machine. "You want something?"

"I didn't bring any money."

Seth smiled. "It's free." He hit the Pepsi button, and with a clunk, a can of soda dropped out.

Teddy pushed Mountain Dew. There was something magical about a soda machine that was free.

A couple of more guys showed up. Seth introduced Teddy, and they all went and crashed on the couches. Everyone wanted to know how he cracked the firewall so quickly.

Everyone was Seth's age or older, and they all wanted to hang out with Teddy. He had never been cool.

CHAPTER 26

The fall turned to winter, the football team got beat in the first round of the playoffs, and Karen's cheerleading efforts turned to basketball.

Vikram and Wendy had started dating. Teddy didn't hang around with them as much because he felt like a third wheel, but it was okay because he spent most of his time hanging out with his new hacker friends.

Over Christmas break, the Alexanders went out to MIT for a visit. Teddy wasn't sure about being so far from home, but after seeing the facilities, he was too excited to worry about a little homesickness.

Before spring classes had even started, Teddy had his application sent off.

Now that Teddy was thirteen and knew where he wanted to go to college, he found high school to be much less stressful.

Both Vikram and Wendy were going to be gone for spring break. Vikram was visiting Stanford, and Wendy's family had a reunion in Cancún.

After breakfast, he rode his bike to the library and locked it up. His timing was perfect, and he hopped on the bus. It took two transfers, but that got him close enough he could walk to the shipping containers he liked to call the hideout.

There were a couple of guys sleeping on the couches, but other than that the place was empty. Teddy didn't mind, he would have the computer pit all to himself.

The door behind the desk, which he had learned led to Neal's apartment, opened up, and Jade came out. "Hey, Teddy," she said and waved to him. "Neal wants to see you."

Teddy didn't say anything. She was in her underwear. He blushed and walked toward her, keeping his eyes on the floor. She said, "You're such a cutie."

Jade put her arm around him and said, "He's in the crow's nest. I'll show you."

She smelled nice.

Behind the door was a spectacular room with hardwood floors, a kitchen, and a bed on one side. Under some shiny silver sheets was Stephanie. Jade took Teddy's hand and led him to another door. It was a stairwell that went up four flights.

The crow's nest was another shipping container with windows all around it. There were a couple of couches, a small refrigerator, and computer with three screens on each end. Neal said, "Teddy, my man, good to see you."

Jade said, "I'm going back to bed."

Teddy said, "Thanks, Jade," keeping his eyes down, but he snuck a look as she walked away.

"Teddy, do you know what I do for a living?"

"I just thought you were really rich."

"I am, but I've also got a security consulting business."

"That's cool."

"Here, come over here, and sit down."

Teddy grabbed a chair.

"Basically, what I do is test company's online defenses against hackers."

"How do you do that?"

"We arrange a day, and they do their best to keep my team from getting into their system."

"You mean they pay you to hack their system?"

"Yes. They know it's coming but not what time, and my fee is based upon my success or not. If we're successful, we get twice as much as if they keep us out."

"So you just have to get into their system, and if you do, you get paid."

"Well, there's a file we need to download. That's the goal."

"What do you do then?"

"I write a detailed report about how we got through their defenses so they can improve and keep their data safe."

"That sounds like a fun job."

Neal laughed and went to the refrigerator. "It is. You want something to drink?"

"Sure."

Neal pulled out a Mountain Dew and tossed it to Teddy. "How would you like to help me out?"

"Sure."

"The pay is great and because I pick the days, we can be flexible with your schedule. It would be nice to have some extra money when you go off to college, wouldn't it?"

Teddy nodded.

"The thing is, I'll want to see you in action a couple of times to make sure you're up to it. There is a lot of money on the line, and it depends upon us getting those files. Does that make sense?"

"What do I do?"

Neal smiled and pulled up a file. "This is what we're going to do."

* * *

For three hours, they planned the attack. Jade and Stephanie joined them when it was time to start. Neal was at one end, Teddy at the other, and Jade and Stephanie used their laptops from the table in the middle.

They began with a denial of service attack to offer a distraction. When Neal said go, Teddy started his part of the plan. It took ninety minutes, but Teddy succeeded in downloading the file just like they planned.

The moment the file was done downloading, Neal took the thumb drive and patted Teddy on the back. Stephanie and Jade both cheered and gave Teddy high-fives.

Neal said, "Teddy, you were great. I knew you could do it. Now, because you're thirteen, I can't technically put you on the payroll, but I'm a man of my word, and I'm going to take care of you." He pulled out an envelope from a drawer and handed it to Teddy. "Now, promise me you'll save some of this for when you go to college."

Teddy opened the envelope. He couldn't believe his eyes, there were ten hundred dollar bills. "This is too much. It only took an hour and a half."

Neal said, "You also spent three hours planning it, and don't forget, we made twice as much because of you. I take care of my people. Let's get some lunch."

Teddy had never had so much fun in his life. They ate sushi, told stories, and laughed a bunch.

On Monday and Wednesday, Neal had consulting jobs, and Teddy helped. Both times, he got envelopes. He wasn't sure why, but he didn't tell his parents about his new job. He put the money in a bank he built out of Lego blocks and hid under his bed.

One thought kept bugging Teddy. It was too much money. He decided he didn't want to help anymore and on Thursday went to tell Neal.

When he got to the hideout there were about twenty people there milling around.

Neal got up from his desk when Teddy walked in and said, "There's my star."

"Hi, Neal."

Everyone looked at Teddy. Neal came over and said, "Saturday is the day. I need everyone to be sharp, rested, and ready to roll."

Teddy said, "Can I talk to you, Neal?"

"Sure, what's on your mind?"

"I don't think I can help on this one."

It got really quiet. Everyone had stopped talking and was just looking at Teddy and Neal. Neal said, "Come on back, let's talk."

Teddy followed Neal back to his apartment. Neal grabbed two Mountain Dews and gave one to Teddy.

They sat at the kitchen table, and Neal asked, "What's going on?"

"Nothing, I just don't think I can make it on Saturday."

"I need you, Teddy. It's important."

"I have to go somewhere with my parents," Teddy lied.

"Where?"

Teddy wasn't ready and stammered a bit. "To see my aunt."

Neal didn't say anything. He got up and paced. After what seemed like forever, Neal said, "I don't think you understand. We can't do this without you. You're my Michael Jordan. You don't want to let down the team, do you?"

Teddy just shrugged.

"Okay, I'm going to be straight with you, Theodore Alexander. You don't have a choice. You're going to be here on Saturday morning by 8:00 am, or you'll regret it."

"I'm sorry, I can't...my aunt..."

"Bullshit. You're in this up to your neck."

Teddy didn't know what he meant.

"You think this is a game?"

"No, it's your consulting."

"Don't pretend you believed that consulting crap. You've been hacking some of the most secure companies in the world all week and downloading...oh... around three million credit card numbers. You're the most wanted hacker in the world right now."

Teddy thought he was going to pass out. Now the money made sense, and it made his stomach churn.

"On Saturday, we're going to take down CitiBank, and you're the key."

"I don't want to take down CitiBank. I'm not a hacker. I didn't know we were..."

Neal put his hand on Teddy's shoulder and said, "Hey, calm down, it's going to be okay. You just need to do this one more time, and then we're closing up shop."

Teddy put his hands in his face. He wanted to cry. In a mere instant, everything that Teddy had ever dreamed of was crumbling before his eyes. He could see his MIT plans shatter and then an even worse thought piled on the rest: what would his parents think?

Neal said, "It's all going to be fine. You get us into CitiBank on Saturday, and then you never have to do it again."

"But won't the police be looking for me?"

"Yes, but if you never do any more hacking, they won't be able to find you."

Teddy was shaking.

"Listen, I know it's a crappy deal. I betrayed you, but I'm sort of an asshole, so now you've learned a valuable lesson. And look at it this way, if you don't help us, my friend will make a call and let the cops know who's been stealing all these credit cards. So, are you going to help me out?"

"Yes, I'll do it."

"Good man."

Teddy got up and walked out. He didn't go straight to the bus stop. He just wandered around for about an hour replaying every moment of the last week. It was so obvious, he didn't know how he couldn't have seen it.

He wished he could go back in time, but time travel wasn't possible. There had to be a way out of this mess.

Teddy went home and made a sandwich for lunch. Both his parents were at work, and he was glad. They would have been able to tell he was in trouble. After a second PB&J, Teddy knew what he had to do.

He got the money from his Lego bank and put it in his backpack. Forty minutes later, he walked into the lobby of the Seattle branch of the FBI.

A scary-looking guy at a desk asked Teddy, "How may we help you, son?"

"I need to talk to one of your agents about a crime."

"What sort of crime?"

"Stolen credit card numbers. It's important."

The man behind the desk picked up the phone and said, "This is Fenton at the front desk, there's a kid down here who wants to talk to someone about stolen credit cards." He hung up the phone and said, "Special Agent Hailey will be with you in a moment. You may take a seat over there."

Teddy's stomach was spinning. His mind was playing all sorts of scenarios, and most of them had the FBI putting him in jail for the rest of his life. He considered running, but then it was too late. Special Agent Hailey had arrived.

She was a nice-looking black woman in a blue suit. Her face looked friendly. She stuck out her hand and said, "Hello, I'm Special Agent Hailey, and I understand you want to discuss some stolen credit card numbers. Do you know someone who's been trying to sell stolen numbers?"

Teddy looked around. "Could we go talk someplace more private, please?"

She smiled and led him to the elevators. They went up to the third floor and then into a conference room. "Would you like some water or a soda?"

"Maybe later. I'm fine now."

"Okay, so what is it you'd like to tell me?"

Teddy's heart was pounding. He had never been so frightened in his whole life. He took a deep breath and said, "I'm the guy you've been looking for."

A perplexed look settled on Hailey's face. "You don't look like any of the most wanted posters I've seen."

"That's because you don't know who I am yet."

"Why don't we back up and you can explain to me why you think the FBI is looking for you."

"Okay, it's a long story, you may want to take notes. Do you need to read me my rights?"

She laughed and said, "Why don't you just tell me what's on your mind."

Teddy gave a sigh. "I want to start by explaining that I'm thirteen years old, but I'm in eleventh grade. I've skipped four grades." Teddy took out his school ID and showed her.

"That's impressive."

"Well, I'm pretty smart, but I'm also really stupid. I got tricked."

"You got tricked, how?"

"I've been learning how to program computers, and I joined a club at school. One of the guys in the club, Seth, introduced me to another guy named Neal. Neal has been teaching me all sorts of stuff, and this week he tricked me into stealing credit card numbers."

Special Agent Hailey seemed to be taking him seriously. She was taking notes.

"He said he was hired as a consultant to try to break into these companies so they could learn where their weaknesses were and they got paid more if we downloaded a special file. He lied to me."

"When did this happen?"

"On Saturday, Monday, and Wednesday."

"Do you mind if I get one of my colleagues?"

"No, I'll wait here."

Teddy sat alone. He could see people hard at work. Special Agent Hailey had walked across the room, and he saw her knock on a wood door. It opened, and she disappeared inside.

A few people who walked past the conference room window looked at Teddy. It made him nervous. He thought about what was going to happen to him. Obviously, he was too young to go to adult prison, but there were still prisons for kids under eighteen years old.

Visions of fights, or more accurately, piles of boys beating and kicking him as he lay on the floor, defenseless, filled Teddy's head. Then he thought about Mr. Chompers. His parents would feed him, but would he understand why Teddy wasn't playing with him anymore.

Special Agent Hailey returned and said, "This is Captain Roberts."

Teddy, fighting back the tears, said, "Hi, sir, I'm Theodore Alexander. I'm here to confess. I don't want to go to jail, but I don't want to be a criminal anymore."

Captain Roberts sat down. "Theodore, it took a lot of bravery to come forward. I'm not ready to send you off to jail just yet. It sounds to me like you're trying to help."

Teddy looked up and with wet eyes said, "I am! They're going after CitiBank on Saturday. Neal said that if I didn't help, he would turn me in, but I don't want to help him steal stuff from millions of people. I decided I'd turn myself in, and maybe you could stop him. He's mean."

"Theodore, the first thing we need to do is to look into your story."

"It's not a story, it happened. Look!" He pulled the envelopes out of his backpack and slid them across the table. "I'm only thirteen. How many thirteen-year-olds have three thousand dollars in cash? This is the money he gave me. I didn't spend any of it."

The captain said, "It's not that I don't believe you, it's that we've not heard of any of attacks this week."

Teddy seemed confused. "You mean I'm not the most wanted hacker in the world?"

The captain slid a yellow legal pad and a pencil across to Teddy. "Here, can you write down the names of the companies and which dates the thefts occurred."

"Are you saying that nobody stole any credit card numbers this week?"

"Sometimes, companies are a little slow to report these types of thefts; other times, they don't even know they've been robbed. It isn't that I don't believe you, it's that we need to look into it a bit more. Understand?"

Teddy wrote down the names and slid it back.

The captain got up and said, "Special Agent Hailey will look into these, and you and I can discuss the case in more detail."

Teddy felt small. "Okay, sir."

Over the next hour, people were coming and going, whispering in the captain's ear, and sliding things in front of him. Teddy described the secret hiding place and drew a diagram.

Three men with computer laptops knocked, and the captain let them in and shook their hands. The older man with white hair said, "This kid is the one who hacked us?"

Teddy lowered his head and said, "I'm sorry. They tricked me."

"How old are you?"

"I'm thirteen, but I'm in eleventh grade."

"These two gentlemen are the head of our IT security. They tell me that you broke through a firewall that we thought was the safest in the world."

"I'm really sorry."

"The thing is, we didn't even notice the files were compromised until about an hour before we got called by our FBI friends here."

The captain said, "Theodore, it seems everything checks out, and though I can't speak for the other two companies, Mr. Preston here isn't as interested in pressing charges as he is in finding out how you did it."

Mr. Preston said, "If you show us how you got in, then as far as I'm concerned, you've done us a favor."

Teddy looked up and asked, "Then you won't send me to jail?"

"Send you to jail?! No, I'd rather give you a job."

One of the other guys set his laptop in front of Teddy and said, "Can you show us how you got in?"

Teddy said, "Neal, Jade, and Stephanie created a distraction with a DOS attack, which is probably why you didn't notice me sneaking in through the back door."

Mr. Preston said, "I wasn't aware we had any back doors."

"Oh, not a real back door. It was just a figure of speech. I meant...here, let me show you."

Teddy started typing, and before long, he had code scrolling on the screen. "Here, this is the first weakness. It doesn't look like a hole until you see this part down here." He scrolled for another sixty pages and pointed. Then he described exactly the type of code he used to get past the firewall.

One of the younger guys said, "This is pure genius."

"Thanks."

Mr. Preston slid his card across the table. "When you've got everything cleared up here, give me a call."

"Yes, sir."

After Mr. Preston and his IT guys left, the captain said, "See, that wasn't so bad. He's not pressing charges...against you anyway. We're going to get the other two companies in here, and I'd bet they'll be just as happy to find out how you did it as Mr. Preston."

"So, I'm not going to jail?"

"You came to us and did the right thing. That matters, and I'd say you're helping us to catch the real criminals, so no, you're not going to jail."

Teddy let out a long sigh.

When 5:00 rolled around, Teddy called home to let his parents know he wasn't going to be there for dinner. It took three more hours to plan how they would stop the plan to get CitiBank. When they were done, Special

Agent Hailey put Teddy's bike in the back of her car and took him home.

She explained, in glowing terms, how Teddy had uncovered a plot that the FBI hadn't seen on their radar and how his actions had helped save tens of millions of dollars.

On Saturday, Teddy hacked CitiBank just as Neal was expecting. When the FBI rolled in and arrested everyone, nobody looked more surprised than Neal. Teddy, who had been told to act like he didn't know what was going on, played the part perfectly. Neal even said he was sorry to Teddy as they put him in the back of a police car.

Even Seth got caught up in the sting, and unfortunately for him, he had just turned eighteen the week before. He was no longer a minor.

Saturday night, Teddy and his parents were guests of Captain Roberts at a dinner in Teddy's honor. All his new FBI friends were there, and Teddy was the hero.

The next day, there was a huge story in the newspaper, but they kept Teddy's name out of it, which was fine with him, he just wanted to get back to school and put the whole thing behind him.

Things didn't work out exactly as he had hoped. Word got out about Teddy's involvement, and when he was at school on Monday, Seth's friends noticed and outed him as a snitch.

Word spread quickly, and by the end of the day the only people who would talk to Teddy were Wendy and Vikram.

Tuesday was much worse.

* * *

The rest of the semester, Teddy kept his eyes on the floor and avoided everyone. Even Vikram and Wendy were getting grief, and he told them it would be better if they just kept their distance. They were both too into each other too much to worry about Teddy, and so he got his wish. He was alone.

Teddy didn't like school much after that. He still loved learning, but he wanted to get on with his life, and that meant college. He spent the summer taking courses so he could graduate at the end of fall semester.

His mother wanted him to wait until the following fall to attend MIT, but he was insistent, and so after classes ended, they went to Massachusetts to get him settled.

Teddy had done some consulting work for each of the companies he had hacked, and they paid him well. It was this money that let him get his own place on campus so he didn't have to live in the dorms. It had been quite a battle with his mother, but he explained that he was in school to do serious work and the distraction of dorm life would be counterproductive.

In truth, he just wanted to be alone.

Without any friends or any distractions, Teddy became a learning machine. A bitterness took hold of him, and he was only happy when he had his nose in a book or when it was Mr. Chompers's floor time.

Teddy achieved outstanding grades and had no problem transitioning from his bachelor's degree into the master's program. His professors liked and respected him; his classmates mostly ignored him unless it was absolutely necessary.

During the four years it took for Teddy to finish both his bachelor of science and his master's degree in physics, he had only one joy other than Mr. Chompers: reading. He devoured books like they were piles of candy at a fat camp. He couldn't get enough. Teddy read everything ever written by Kipling, Nabokov, Turgenev, Tolstoy, Falkner, and other greats and then turned to more contemporary authors like J.K Rowling, Tolkien, and Elmore Leonard.

The last week of school before he graduated, Teddy spent a lot of time thinking. His course work was done, and there didn't seem to be anything left to do but get ready for going to grad school for a PhD in theoretical physics. It troubled him some.

Physics was his great love, and books were a close second, but there was one subject he dearly wanted to understand. Teddy wanted a girlfriend.

The last four years, despite his best effort to keep his head down, had been a constant reminder that he was missing something. Couples on benches, holding hands, Friday night revelers pouring out of bars, and even Saturday morning students lumbering across campus in their walk of shame, all were constant reminders that he was not only alone but might just stay that way for the rest of his life.

He had one professor who had a distinguished career, had published many articles, and was greatly respected by his peers, who had never married. As far as everyone knew, he had never even been on a date. He ate ham sandwiches on wheat bread at his desk every day and walked home alone every night. Teddy admired him, but also feared he was a ghost of future Christmas that needed to be avoided at all cost.

Something needed to be done. In his typical analytical fashion, Teddy looked at the issue and found the core problem. He had never learned how to be a boy, and now he was about to be a young man. Surely, one couldn't pull that off without being a boy first, but since that ship had sailed, he decided he would give being a young man a chance before it was too late.

CHAPTER 27

Teddy hadn't been happy in over four years. The Alexanders sat at dinner, and Teddy was full of smiles. His parents assumed it was because he'd just got his master's degree, and they both gushed about how proud they were of him.

"Mom and Dad, I've made a decision about my future."

Mr. Alexander raised an eyebrow and asked, "That sounds as if you're changing course. Have you burnt out on physics?"

"No, I love physics, but you know what?"

Mrs. Alexander asked, "What?

"Physics isn't going anywhere."

Mrs. Alexander asked, "Are you going somewhere?"

"I think I am, though I'm not sure where yet."

Mrs. Alexander said, "Your father and I were thinking we might all take a cruise, perhaps Greece?"

"That would be fun, I'd like that, but that's not what I'm talking about. I want to spend the next two years of my life in other pursuits. I think I want to do something frivolous."

Mr. Alexander said, "I think you've earned it."

Mrs. Alexander asked, "You really have, Teddy dear. What are your plans?"

"I want to spend time doing something for me. A journey I'll absolutely love even though it won't have any value to society or any redeeming quality. It's completely worthless, but I'm going to do it. I'm going to get a PhD in literature."

Mr. Alexander laughed and said, "I don't know that I qualify a PhD in literature as completely worthless."

Teddy rolled his eyes and said, "Dad, it's a degree in reading and making up things about the author's intent that can't be proved through scientific method. It's for people who can't do math. But I like books, and it will be fun not to have to think for two years."

Mrs. Alexander laughed and said, "You'll be the most well-read Nobel Prize winner ever."

"I do like books."

They laughed and enjoyed dinner. Teddy talked about all the places he was considering. He was most excited about living in the dorms as an eighteen-year-old. "It's going to be a little scary at first because I'm not good at making friends."

His mother started to object, and Teddy held up a finger and said, "I have plenty of data from the last four years, Mother, don't make me show you."

She just shook her head.

"As I was saying, I'm smart, and it is just a matter of paying attention and seeing how the other kids do it. I'll get the hang of being eighteen in no time."

Mr. Alexander said, "That's a great way to look at it. Every problem has a solution."

Teddy's parents listened to their son lay out all his plans. It was a great evening.

A happy child is all they ever wanted.

* * *

It took a few weeks of scouring the Internet, making lists, and considering pros and cons, but finally Teddy made his choice. He would attend Beckerston College. It was a small liberal arts school, had what seemed like a good staff, and would be a perfect place for him to achieve his goals.

The application process didn't take long. He heard back almost immediately by phone and received his acceptance letter a few days later. Teddy's letters of reference, which included his Nobel Prize-winning friend, did the trick.

Teddy had lost touch with Vikram and Wendy. He found Vikram easily enough, as he was working on his master's degree at Stanford. Vikram brought him up to speed on Wendy.

It seems Wendy had joined the army after high school to take advantage of the GI Bill, but had loved it and decided to make a career of the military. She was married to a guy who owned a hardware store that was three years older than she. Vikram and Wendy had remained good friends after they broke up, and he spoke highly of her husband.

Teddy was pleased that everyone was doing well. The rest of the summer, he and Vikram emailed each other a couple of times per week.

When the day finally arrived, Teddy and his parents piled in the car for the two-day drive to school. He drove most of the way because it wasn't something he got to do very often. When they arrived at Beckerston, it was late on the evening before he could move into the dorms. Teddy figured if he got in early he could start watching how everyone acted and start to figure stuff out. He didn't sleep that well.

The pulled into the Hilltop dorms at 8:00 a.m., and the place was packed. It seemed everyone else had the same idea.

The first ten words out of Teddy's mouth that day were "Hey." All around, the unbridled optimism of youth were ready to get their education on...or at the very least, drink beer until they puked. By Teddy's calculation, it seemed the latter was more likely.

Teddy's mind was racing. He had done some research on how kids his age talk, and for the first time in his life he couldn't remember any of it. If there had been a quiz, he would have failed. The thought made him chuckle.

It didn't take long to get his stuff into room N125. It looked like his roommate was already moved in because there was already stuff on the walls and everything.

Teddy's mom had been instructed multiple times that crying wouldn't be allowed. He could tell it was hard on her, but he gave his mom a hug and whispered, "Good job. You can cry in the car if you want."

She laughed and said, "Okay, I will."

Mr. Alexander handed Teddy some money and said, "I know you don't need it, but spend this on something you don't need."

"Thanks, Dad."

And with that, they were gone. It was strange how this day was so much different than when he had been fourteen at MIT. On that day, he had been escorted around by a tenured professor, people already knew who he was, and since he was living by himself, there weren't lots of people to meet. This was more than a little bit scary, but that was the point. It was also exciting.

Teddy unpacked his clothes and put them away neatly. He didn't know if his roommate was neat or not, and though he preferred to be tidy, he was willing to guess Billy wasn't that way.

Billy was a sophomore on the baseball team. He was six foot three, a pitcher, and a pretty fair hitter, too. Teddy had done his research.

Billy walked in with two women in tow and bellowed, "Teddy Alexander, welcome to college!"

"Hey, Billy. It's nice to meet you."

"Not half as nice as it is to meet Allison and Jennifer. Allison and Jennifer, this is my new roommate, Teddy. He's a genius."

They both smiled and said, "And cute as a button."

Billy set down the twelve-pack he was carrying and said, "Let's get this mayhem started."

Both girls squealed and took beers. Teddy had never had a beer and wasn't sure what to do, but the voice in his head said not taking a beer would be the stupidest thing he had ever done, so when Billy held out a beer, Teddy took it.

It tasted awful.

Teddy had no idea why everyone wanted beer, especially at that hour of the morning, but he was on their turf now, and he intended to learn. When he got a minute, he whispered to Billy, "I'm not much of a drinker."

"I know."

"How did you know?"

"I Googled you, dude. Anyone that already has two degrees by eighteen isn't spending a lot of time drunk off their ass."

"About that, I sort of want to keep my..."

"Brains?"

"Yes, if you could not tell people about MIT that would be great."

Billy shook his head and said, "You're The Man. If you don't use that MIT shit as your opening line to get bitches, I'm going to be sorely disappointed in you."

"It's just that I want to be a normal eighteen-year-old."

"Look at the bodies on those two," Billy said, nodding toward Allison and Jennifer. "You ever had anything like that?"

"No," Teddy sighed and added, "I know less about girls than I do about beer."

"Then that's why the college gods have made you my roommate. I don't know much...you can check my grades, but there are two things I do know. One, how to throw a filthy split finger fastball and two, how to make women swoon."

Teddy looked at him askew.

"Oh yes, I said swoon. I'm not afraid to bust out a vocabulary word now and again."

"Billy, I think you may be The Man."

"I think you need another beer."

Teddy's head was spinning a little after the first one. If it hadn't been for the second one, though, he might not have ever danced with Allison. He was awful, but not embarrassingly so, and she didn't seem to notice.

By 10:00 a.m., he had his first college puke. Teddy was clever about it, though, and went to a bathroom on a different floor. It went quickly, he rinsed his mouth out with water, and then returned to the room to find his toothbrush. It was time to pace himself, or he would be dead before his first class on Monday.

It was awesome.

People were running around, making new friends, flirting, and all of this before noon. Billy explained that he generally ate at the training table, but was going to show Teddy the ropes. "You can go down the east or west lines, they are both supposed to be the same, but the west line has Becky."

"Who's Becky?"

"She's a middle-age woman with two kids that wants to get busy with Wigman."

"Who's Wigman?"

"He's in the room next to us, and he's a junior. He's been flirting with her for a couple of years. You'll meet him later; he's at his girlfriend's today, meeting her parents."

"I'm sorry, but I don't understand the correlation between Wigman, Becky, and my lunch."

"You will."

They had bacon cheeseburgers, and Billy got his and said, "Hey, Becky, this is my new roommate, Teddy."

Teddy said, "Hello."

"Why, hello there, welcome to Beckerston." She put a burger on his tray and then slid four extra pieces of bacon in next to it with a wink.

"See," Billy said, hitting Teddy in the shoulder and added, "I told you Becky would take care of us."

Becky said, "You be good boys."

"Maybe for a couple more hours, but then I can't make any promises," Billy said with a wink.

Teddy smiled, lowered his voice, and said, "Thanks for the extra bacon, Becky."

"You're welcome, Teddy," she whispered back.

Billy made a beeline for a table filled with girls. It seemed like he knew half of them. Everyone got introduced to Teddy, and he did his best to remember names, but he forgot about half of them by the time he finished his burger. Teddy didn't talk much. He didn't need to. Billy was telling stories and jokes like a talk show host. The girls were eating it up. Teddy was taking mental notes.

After lunch, they went back to the room, and Billy suggested Teddy go slowly on the beer until later. "Just nurse this one, and you'll look cool."

People came and went. There were lots of baseball players, and eventually Wigman showed up. They could hear people shouting his name all down the hall. Wigman was blond, ripped, and jovial in a badass sort of way. Teddy liked him.

The three of them played Xbox all afternoon. Teddy wasn't very good at it, but he did hit one home run, which earned him a couple of high-fives.

By the time they were ready for dinner, there were three parties they knew about, and Wigman suggested they go to the bars first.

Teddy said, "I'm only eighteen."

Wigman said, "So, what we have here is a man without a fake ID. Is that correct, young man?"

"Yes."

Wigman made a call, and ten minutes later a guy who was six foot six, had black hair, and weighed about 270 pounds showed up and handed over his driver's license. "You can use mine."

Teddy looked up at the towering linebacker and said, "I'm not sure I see the family resemblance."

Everyone howled. It was the first time Teddy had got a laugh. He would remember that moment for the rest of his life.

Wigman said, "Listen, don't worry about it. You just hand the license to the guy at the door, look him straight in the eye, and say, 'How much is cover'?"

"Yes, but I'm small and nerdy, and he's huge."

"It's all about attitude, Teddy my man," Billy said. "Trust Wigman, he knows stuff."

"I do know stuff. My major is stuff. Heck, I'm even getting a minor in stuff."

Teddy said, "Okay" and thanked the linebacker.

CHAPTER 28

His first day at Beckerston wasn't even done, and he had two friends, a hookup on the food line, and had learned how to play baseball on the Xbox. He had even done some drinking without any terrible consequences. It was a banner day.

They ordered pizza for dinner, sausage and mushroom, and more of the baseball team started to hang out. Billy and Wigman made sure everyone knew who Teddy was, and it seemed their seal of approval was enough for him to be instantly accepted and one of the gang.

If he were doing a scientific study (and really, he was), Teddy would have concluded that this is what it felt like to be cool. The physicists he had been in school with were definitely not cool. Though, Teddy did have to admit that he hadn't made an effort to really get to know them. Maybe they were cool in a different way.

Most of his new friends were in their second year at Beckerston. They knew which bars were fun and which parties would have the best girls. It was Wigman who had said, "The Sig Eps always have the best women at their shindigs," though Teddy wasn't sure of the criteria Wigman used to judge.

As he was getting ready to go out, he thought about these things. What made a "best woman"? His mental list went brains, liked books, not too tall, nice smile, and then finally, had good parents. It seemed definitive, but to be sure he went next door to ask Wigman who was blow-drying his hair and singing to AC/DC.

Wigman turned off the hair dryer and screamed, "For those about to rock..."

Teddy made a salute sign, as he figured that's what Wigman was after. It was the fifth time he'd heard the song in the last hour.

Wigman screamed, "We salute you," and then turned off the song. "You're looking sharp, T-Dawg."

"I'm not sure I can pull off T-Dawg as a nick name."

"You can pull off any Dog...you're the man."

Billy wandered in and agreed. "You really are the man."

"I've never been the man before."

Billy raised an eyebrow and asked, "What about at that other place that I'm not supposed to mention, that you went to...twice...while we were all trying to lose our virginity in high school?"

Wigman asked, "What other place?"

Billy looked at Teddy.

Teddy said, "I kind of want to keep it on the down low, okay?"

Wigman said, "No problem."

"I sort of already went to college."

Billy said, "He's already got a bachelor's and a master's in physics...from...wait for it...M-I-motherfucking-T."

Wigman said, "No Way, that's freaking awesome. I suck at science. You really are the man!"

"Thanks, but I really want to just be a normal freshman if that's all right."

Billy said, "I hate to point out the obvious, but you are here to get a PhD in literature. The other students may not be as smart as you, but they will figure it out that you're a clever monkey."

Wigman screamed, "Teddy is the Monkey King!"

"I'm not sure I like that nickname either."

Wigman and Billy both started chanting, "Monkey King, Monkey King, Monkey King."

It was hard not to get enthused about a nickname when Wigman gave it to you.

A half hour later, they were walking out of Hilltop dorm and headed to the bars. Their first stop was a place called Edgar's Pit. There wasn't a doorman so Teddy didn't need to use his fake ID. He was relieved.

The subject of what makes a "best woman" had been lost in all of the "Monkey King" chanting, but it was still on Teddy's mind. He wasn't really sure how to talk to women. Billy and Wigman didn't have any problems in this area. They were both silver-tongued salesmen from hell and the ladies were buying.

Billy bought a couple of pitchers, and the three of them grabbed a booth. The buzz from the morning beers was long gone, and Teddy eased his way into his fourth beer of the day.

Wigman said, "Now, since you're a rookie in hanging with us, it's probably best you take a few precautions, Monkey King."

"Precautions from what?"

"From getting smashed and passing out by ten. Just remember it's the first inning. You need to pace yourself and...this is key...work a few glasses of water into the mix. They'll help you bounce back tomorrow."

Billy said, "Hangovers suck."

"So if I drink water I won't be hung over?"

"Oh no, you're going to feel like crap, but you won't feel like death. You'll thank me."

"Is it worth it?"

Wigman jumped in and said, "That's one, rookie."

"One what?"

"One stupid question. When you get to three, there's a punishment."

Billy said, "See those two women in the skintight shirts that highlight their..."

Teddy said, "fitness."

Wigman and Billy both roared.

Wigman said, "Let me tell you what I'd like to do with a pair of fitness like those, I'd..." His phone rang, and he said, "Be right back."

Billy said, "Be sure to tell Trish what you wanted to do with that girl's fitness."

"Who's Trish?"

"That's Wigman's girlfriend. She's cool."

"Is Allison your girlfriend?"

"Well, there, we are sort of in a gray area."

"What do you mean?"

"It depends on who you ask."

"I'm asking you."

"Then I'd say no, she is not my girlfriend, but don't tell her I said that."

"Are you seeing someone else, too?"

"Let's just say I have a number of female friends who are not averse to spending some naked time with me...if you know what I mean."

"You don't need to go to MIT to know what you mean...basically...YOU'RE The Man!"

Billy gave him a quiet little fist bump and took a sip of his beer.

Wigman returned and sat down.

"So, is Trish checking up on you?"

"No! Well, yes, but she just called to say she'd meet us at The Palace later."

Teddy asked, "What's The Palace?"

"Only the greatest sports bar in the world," Wigman said and raised his hands as if in reverence to a sports bar deity.

Billy raised his hands too and began what could only be described as Gregorian chant.

"They have TVs everywhere, but not just so you can sit in a different spot and watch the same game, they have all the big games spread throughout the bar. People come from miles around to watch college and pro sports."

Billy jumped in and added, "You see, if you're a fan of the Washington Huskies..."

"I love the Huskies," Teddy said.

"I figured you might. Well, there are probably a few other Huskies fans in the area, and they will come in and look for the tag that says Washington vs. Stanford.

If it says Stanford vs. Washington, then you know that those fans are going to be cheering for the Cardinals."

Wigman said, "It's the same with the NFL, NBA, MLB, whatever the event they've got the place divided up so one can hang out with their peeps."

"It sounds awesome."

"And the waitresses have ample...fitness," said Wigman with a wink.

A couple of girls came over and joined them. Teddy introduced himself, but before he could get their names, another guy from the baseball team was bringing them more beer.

It was starting to get loud.

Wigman started to tell stories, and Teddy was happy to just sit and listen.

They were all just finishing up their beers and about to head over to The Palace when a guy they called Scooter rushed up to the table. Teddy had met him earlier in the day, but all he remembered is that Scooter was the shortstop.

Scooter said, "El Grande is back!"

Wigman said, "Nooooo...I thought we had more time."

Billy said, "I heard he wasn't going to be here until Sunday night."

Scooter said, "He's back, and he's already got two people."

Wigman said, "Fuck. I thought I'd get one weekend without worrying about having A Hand."

Billy said, "That fucker stalked me for an entire day last spring. I let my guard down for one minute, and bam, right in the ass. I'm glad I didn't have to pitch that day, I mostly just stood around in the bull pen."

Teddy asked, "Who's El Grande?"

Wigman put his hand on Teddy's shoulder. "He is the most offensive, awful, slob you'll ever love...and hate."

Billy said, "He used to play offensive tackle here, but blew out his knee as a sophomore. That was four years ago, and he just keeps coming back."

"Is he working on a master's degree now?"

Everyone laughed.

Wigman said, "I heard he's still trying to get enough credits to be a senior."

Scooter said, "The thing is, he invented this game, and it is a literal pain in the ass."

Teddy looked a little concerned, as did the girls, but they were all ears.

Wigman said, "It's like this. If you're on the baseball or football team, then you're playing. If you're friends with guys on either team, then you're playing..."

"What if I don't want to?"

"You don't have a choice. El Grande will target you extra hard if you try not to play."

Billy said, "The rules are simple. If you have a beer you must be drinking it in your off hand."

"What's my off hand?"

"Are you right- or left-handed?"

"Right."

"Then from this day forward, you must always drink with your left hand."

"Okay," Teddy said and switched the nearly empty beer to his left hand.

Billy continued, "The other thing is you must always have a beer...or...a hand."

"What do you mean?"

"If you don't have a beer or an open hand covering your ass, then anyone playing the game can kick you."

Wigman said, "And these guys kick hard. Heck, I got booted by the kicker once, and his career long was fifty-nine yards."

"So as long as I keep an open hand or have a beer, I'm okay."

"Yes, but there is one more thing...and this is important. You need to know about the Benny Roll."

"What's that?"

"It's clearly stated in the Boot Game rules that if there is any beer in the glass or container the person is holding, and they are booted, then the person who was the offending kicker is subjected to a penalty kick."

"Okay, but what's this Benny Roll thing? Is it a type of kick?"

"No, it's what you do with your glass," Wigman said and grabbed what appeared to be an empty glass. He rolled it between his hands and held it over his open mouth. A single drop of beer dropped.

Scooter said, "That means you were holding a beer, even if it is only a drop. If I had kicked you thinking you were holding an empty beer, then you and anyone who witnessed the personal foul would get a free penalty kick." Scooter bent over and put his hands on his knees and continued, "I have to stay like this and just take it."

Billy said, "You don't want to have to endure penalty kicks. People are brutal, but not with just the kicks. They will line up and take two or three swings at you without connecting...just to warm up. It's the anticipation that's the worst."

Wigman said, "The bottom line is El Grande is back, and you better have a hand or a beer if you want to be able to sit through class on Monday."

One of the girls asked, "It's just guys, right?"

Wigman said, "If you want to run with this crowd, missy, you better have a beer or a hand. El Grande doesn't care if you've got a set of balls or not...it's booting season, and he's got a size 14 just waiting for action."

Neither girl knew what to make of this game, but they didn't look scared either. Teddy decided the rules were simple and he could manage to keep a hand when he wasn't drinking a beer. It was a stupid game, but being part of something so ridiculous was exactly what he had wanted from this time at college.

* * *

They moved as a band of brothers (and sisters) hoping to make it to The Palace without an El Grande sighting.

"You'll be able to hear him before you see him," Warned Billy.

Wigman said, "His battle cry is 'Fuck Off,' and his voice carries."

Scooter said, "El Grande was once arrested pissing on a fire truck while the firefighters were battling a blaze. He told the arresting officer to fuck off, and it didn't go over well.

Halfway to the bar, the two girls saw some of their friends and broke ranks. It was just the four of them.

The group was pretty well buzzed, but they all had hands covering their six.

A rush of nervousness swept through Teddy as they reached The Palace. Two huge guys with tattoos were at the door. One was checking IDs, and the other was taking the cover charge.

Teddy looked at his ID and started to sweat. He remembered what he'd been told, to just be confident and everything would be fine, but there wasn't a single thing on his fake ID that resembled him.

Billy and Scooter were the first in, and then it was Teddy's turn. He handed the driver's license to the bouncer and said, "How much is cover this evening, sir?"

In his head it sounded okay, but when Teddy heard it out loud, he sounded like a nervous underage English butler. It did not sound confident.

The bouncer said, "Five bucks. Pay him."

Teddy gave the other guy a five, and the bounder gave one more look at the ID He said, "Great game last week."

Teddy just said, "Thanks." He had no idea what the bouncer was talking about.

Wigman didn't show an ID or pay cover. He just gave the bouncer a chest bump and walked in.

Teddy asked Billy, "What did he mean by 'good game'?"

Billy laughed. He plays on the football team with your ID. In fact, they're roommates.

"Did you know he would be the bouncer?"

"Yes."

"Why didn't you tell me?"

Scooter jumped in and said, "Because we wouldn't have got to hear you say, 'How much is cover, sir?' like a teenage girl."

Wigman patted him on the back and said through his laughter, "You did fine, I didn't think you sounded like a teenage girl at all. I'd have put you at least twenty years old."

Teddy couldn't help but laugh. He had been teased plenty in his life. This was the first time it wasn't mean. The words were the same, but the faces were all smiles. Teddy bought the first round.

They found themselves a table near the dance floor. It seemed that everyone in the bar knew Teddy's new friends. People came over said hi and asked about their summers. It seemed the one constant was people were thrilled to be back at school.

The music was loud, and Teddy wasn't good with small talk, so he just watched and drank his beer...with his off hand. He was careful about that point.

Trish showed up with her roommate who, it turned out, was the Allison he'd met that morning. Trish made Wigman dance with her despite his protests. Everyone sided with Trish on that one.

Allison sat next to Teddy and asked, "Are you ready to drink your face off?"

Teddy was pretty sure he wasn't at all ready but said, "Yes!"

Allison had brown hair, brown eyes, and great cheekbones. Teddy thought she was more than just pretty but was remarkable looking. She was easy to talk to and didn't seem to care that he was younger. She was twenty and from Greenville, Ohio.

Allison asked, "What are you going to major in, Teddy?"

"Literature."

"What does one do with a degree in literature?"

Teddy didn't want to mention that he was going for a PhD and said, "I would think one proudly hangs it on their office wall."

Allison laughed. "Is it good for anything else?"

"I could write a scholarly tome that nobody would read."

"Why would you do that?"

"I hear that next year book nerds are going to be the new sports gods in dating circles."

"You know, I had heard something about that."

"Tall, dark, and handsome is going to be replaced by..."

"Average, brown, and bespectacled. You will be getting some glasses that you wear on the end of your nose, won't you?"

"I will now."

Somebody at the bar yelled something about a special on Jell-O shots, and Allison jumped up. "Come with me, we're getting shots for everyone."

Teddy did as he was told.

Things got a little blurry after that. El Grande made a big entrance, but only Scooter got caught without a beer or a hand. Teddy was in a state of warm and fuzzy until the bar closed. There was an after-hours party, but the only thing he remembered from that was the person had sixteen TV dinners in their freezer and they were all fish. It made Teddy chuckle.

Day one of Teddy's new life was a huge success.

CHAPTER 29

Teddy woke up to a woman he didn't recognize sneaking out of their dorm room. Billy said, "I hope we weren't too loud."

"I didn't hear a thing. In fact, I don't remember coming home."

"You were super hammered."

"Did I do anything stupid?"

"No, but it was your first night, you'll do better next time."

Teddy sat up in bed and experienced his first hangover.

Billy laughed. "How you feeling, buddy?"

"The world seems gray, cold, and evil. I may just go back to bed until Monday."

"Not a chance. Hit the showers, rookie. We've got a full day ahead."

Teddy grabbed his towel and shower bucket and followed Billy to the floor's showers. It was 10:00 a.m., and it seemed they were the first ones up. "Why are we the only ones up?"

"I'm a morning person."

"I don't know you that well, but I'm pretty sure that if I were making a list of things I hate about you, morning person would be at the top."

Billy seemed to like the "Angry Hungover Teddy."

"We need to get you in shape for next weekend."

"What's next weekend?"

"The first football game of the year, and that means tailgating."

"Why don't we just not stay out so late on Friday to make Saturday morning less painful?"

"That's two."

Teddy could see how that was a stupid question and regretted asking it. "Don't they reset after a while?"

"Nope, it's a lifetime tally. The next one results in a penalty of some sort."

Teddy thought about this while he washed his hair. The warm water made him feel three points better...on a one to eight hundred scale. He was currently at fifteen.

Billy explained as they walked back from the showers that if Teddy needed to get any stuff for class, that he should get it done by 3:00, because that's when practice tailgate began.

They got dressed and swung by the C300s to find Wigman, who wasn't in his room. Billy guessed he had stayed with Trish.

They knocked on C302. Trish said, "It's open."

Trish was at her desk, rubbing a towel over her head. Wigman was still in the bottom bunk with a pillow over his head. Trish asked, "Could you do something about Mr. Lazy Pants?"

Billy kicked the bed, "Come on, it's time to get up."

"Fuck you."

"We're getting some breakfast. If we don't hurry, all the bacon will be gone."

"You say that every time."

"And what happened the one time you ignored me?"

Billy looked at Teddy and said, "Bacon is his Kryptonite...but in reverse. He loves it."

"I love bacon, too."

"Everyone loves bacon."

Trish said, "I don't."

Wigman said, "You're a vegetarian, you're not people."

"That's one."

Billy laughed.

Teddy said, "That wasn't a question."

Billy said, "They have their own penalty system. Two more, and Wigman will be back in his room tonight."

Teddy noted that Allison's bed hadn't been slept in or maybe she had got up early and made it, he thought optimistically.

His optimism was shattered when she came in wearing the same clothes as the night before.

Wigman said, "Good morning, sunshine, how was your morning walk of shame?"

"It was lovely. He made me coffee."

Billy said, "This wasn't that Craig guy you were talking to at The Palace?"

Allison said, "It was not...well...I don't think so. What did Craig look like?"

Billy said, "Sort of a mix of goth and hipster, if that is even possible."

Allison started laughing.

"Was it him?"

"I think it was, but I was calling him Greg," she said with a shrug and disappeared into her closet.

Teddy wanted to say something clever to fit in, but he didn't have any good banter for this situation.

Allison came out of the closet in a sweatshirt and shorts and said, "Okay, I need to get some bacon and eggs down my gullet soon, or I'm going to get bitchy."

Trish scoffed at the mention of bacon.

Everyone but Trish headed down for breakfast.

Allison sat across from Teddy and asked, "How you feeling, Monkey King?"

"How did you know about that?"

Wigman and Billy laughed.

Allison said, "When you were slamming your last beer at The Palace, they were chanting it."

"Thanks, guys."

Billy said, "We're here to help."

"It's not the best nickname."

Allison said, "It's better than what they used to call me."

"You didn't like soggy?"

Allison held her fork out in a threatening manner and said, "Don't make me tell Trish you earned a penalty at breakfast...Wigman."

"Fuck, I hate the penalty system."

Teddy laughed. "You've got to tell me why they called you soggy. I mean, there has to be a story."

"It's not a pretty story."

Billy said, "Don't be a pussy."

"Last year's homecoming game started at eleven o'clock. Unlike these pussies, I was at our tailgating spot by 7 a.m. Trish and I were holding down the spot because we're awesome. There may have been a cooler filled with Budweiser, and I may have got after it a little more aggressively than a proper lady should."

Wigman laughed. "Proper lady."

She pointed her fork aggressively and then continued, "By 9:00, things were in full swing, and I was already several sheets to a northerly breeze when a couple of Sig Eps decided to hold an impromptu wet T-shirt contest. Normally, I wouldn't even consider such entering a contest that so belittles women...but...sometimes these girls have a mind of their own."

Billy said, "In Allison's defense, the Sig Eps were offering a $250 bar tab at The Palace."

"A girl's got to eat...well, drink at least. Though they do have wings. Anyway, I was wearing a T-shirt, but hadn't really thought things through because I was not wearing...well..."

Billy jumped in and said, "They sprayed the contestants down, and Allison was very soggy, the water was obviously chilly, and..."

"And I won!"

Teddy held up his orange juice and said, "To victory and nicknames."

Billy and Wigman toasted, and Allison aimed her fork at Teddy and said, "I know where you live, Monkey King, that name has been retired."

"Understood. Still, you got the win."

"Oh, I did, and we tore it up that night at The Palace." She raised her drink box to join the toast.

Billy said, "After we eat, Wigman and I are going to get the keg for practice."

Teddy said, "I still need to get some of my books for Monday."

Allison said, "Monkey, you're with me. Do you know what you need?"

"I think so. I made a list."

"Good, I need to shower off my Friday night shame. I'll swing by your room."

Allison got up and left.

Teddy wasn't sure about more drinking, but he definitely liked the idea of spending time with Allison. She told a good story.

CHAPTER 30

Allison knocked on the door. "Teddy, are you ready?"

"Yes, Allison, it should be fun."

"Did you just mock my rhyme by answering in rhyme?"

"I thought it would be fine, at least I'm not a mime."

"Come on, Mr. Mocky Pants. Do you know the books you need?"

"I do. I've made a list."

They headed down the N100s and out the door at the end of the hall. Allison veered to the right, which was headed to the woods. Teddy asked, "Where are you going?"

"It's a secret shortcut called the Ho Chi Minh Trail."

A few feet into the forest, a well-trodden path wrapped around a large tree and then came to a steep hill. The path wove between a couple of large boulders and then over some jagged rocks. It was obvious the shortcut wasn't a well-kept secret. Four other people were coming up the trail. One of them knew Allison and said, "Hola."

At the bottom of the trail, the trees continued on for a couple of hundred yards, and then it emptied out behind the football stadium. On the other side of the stadium, across the parking lot, was the engineering building. Allison said, "I know a second shortcut through engineering."

The engineering building was the largest on campus, having been donated by a former student who had done well. The actual Engineering Department at Beckerston College was relatively small, but the building was a massive labyrinth.

Allison said, "Most people wouldn't try to get through the other side, but I dated a guy who practically lived here last year, and I know the way."

Teddy followed her up to the second floor, down a hall, and into a huge lecture theater. She ran down the steps and up onto the stage. Teddy was dallying and said, "This is an impressive lecture hall."

"Try to keep up, Monkey."

Teddy did as he was told. Allison crossed the stage and went backstage. Behind a stack of tables, there was an emergency exit. When she pushed the door, Teddy braced for an alarm, but nothing happened.

The door led to another hall that went straight to the other side of the engineering building. They were through the maze. Allison said, "Someday, I'll show you the non-shortcut way to get here. It's amazing how much the theater saves us."

"Cool."

College Books was just across the street. "Let me see your list," Allison said.

Teddy pulled the piece of notebook paper out of his pocket. "I need some school supplies, too."

"School supplies...what...are we getting you ready for, your first day of grade school?"

"You mock me."

"I owed you," she said and looked at the list. "I like your choice of pens. Uni-balls are excellent. This way."

Allison grabbed a basket, handed it to Teddy, and picked up another one for herself. She lingered at the magazine stand, thought better of it, and said, "I need to stay focused. Okay, first stop, the art supplies in the back. They'll have the pens you wanted and the oil paints I need."

"You're an art student?"

"I'm a design student."

Teddy got the pens and then picked up a set of drawing pencils and a sketchbook.

"Are you taking an art class?"

"No, but I used to like drawing."

"Art supplies are like my crack. Every time I come here, I spend money like a Kardashian on Rodeo Drive."

"I need to get a copy of Ernest Hemingway's To Have and Have Not and Rudyard Kipling's Kim."

"Oh, you will not be buying your books here."

"Of course, that would be silly of me to think I might buy my books for college at College Books. I'm such a rookie."

"You're such a monkey."

"I'm the Monkey King."

Allison bought a psych book, a book about online marketing, and then doubled back to the art section to grab a couple of brushes and a French curve set.

They paid and walked down the street. Allison said, "I love this bookshop. Northern Lights is great, they'll have both books you need. They also have a wonderful orange tabby named Sinbad."

"I love a bookshop cat."

"All bookstores should have a cat or two."

Just inside the door was a desk, and on the desk, behind a nameplate that read, "Manager: Sinbad" On a note card taped to the front of a wicker basket where the manager was currently napping, it read, I'll be right with you...unless I'm in a meeting (napping). My assistant, Sarah, will be glad to help you, too.

Sarah looked up and asked, "May I help you find anything?"

"Could you point me toward Ernest Hemingway?"

As if on cue, Sinbad woke up, stood, arched his back and let out a meow.

Allison and Teddy both heaped love and chin scratches on the manager. A moment later, Sinbad hopped off the counter and headed down the hall. Sarah said, "It seems Sinbad is going to show you where to find Hemingway."

Teddy pointed and said, "Follow that cat."

They did, and sure enough Sinbad hopped up into a windowsill right next to a shelf with the book Teddy needed. He opened the cover and started to read. Three pages in, and Teddy was bored. Meh, not every book can be good.

Allison and Sinbad were bonding.

They left, and Teddy said, "Northern Lights is going to be one of my favorite places on campus."

"I know! I love it here. I should have showed you, but they have really comfy couches upstairs in the back."

"Okay, what now?"

"How do you feel about coffee?"

"I like it!"

"Let's go to Sigma Cuppa Joe," she said, giving a nod down the street.

Teddy started off.

"What are you doing?"

"It's not this way?"

"When you're walking with a lady down the street, a gentleman positions himself between the street and the woman."

Teddy stopped, took a step backward, two steps left, and said, "My bad."

"That's better."

"Does your boyfriend walk where you tell him?"

"I don't have a boyfriend."

"Oh, I thought you stayed at his..."

"He was just a hookup. Did you see his abs?"

"I didn't, I'm more of a calves guy," he said as he opened the door and held it for Allison.

"I would have never guessed."

The place was packed, but there were only two people in front of them. Teddy wasn't as big a coffee drinker as he might have let on. Allison ordered first. When the barista asked what he wanted, Teddy said, "What do you recommend?"

"The double mocha espresso is my favorite."

"Great suggestion. I'll try it."

"What's your name?"

Allison said, "His name is Monkey."

The barista wrote Monkey on the cup and smiled at Teddy. Teddy set down his books and took out his wallet to pay and said, "I've got them both."

Allison said, "You don't need to do that."

"I owe you for my careless disregard for your safety that almost resulted in your tragic death. What is the sidewalk death rate on campus?"

"It's a shocking number. I'd rather not think about it. Thanks."

They found a small table, and Allison said, "So, what's the deal? Why are you studying literature? You seem more like a science geek to me."

"I like books."

"Yeah, but what are you going to do with it?"

"Didn't we cover this? I'll put it on my wall."

"For a job, Monkey Boy."

"It's Monkey King."

"What are you going to do for a job, Monkey King?"

"I plan on taxing my monkey minions."

"I'm being serious."

"I'm not actually planning on doing anything with it. I just want to study books in great depth. When I'm done, I'll go back to school and get a PhD in theoretical physics."

"How are you going to get into grad school for physics if you get a bachelor's in literature?"

Teddy looked down. He was a little embarrassed, but he liked Allison and decided to tell her the truth.

"I sort of want to keep this quiet."

"Keep what quiet?"

"What I'm about to tell you."

Allison put her hand on her chest and said, "I swear I can keep a secret."

"I'm not getting a bachelor's in literature, I'm here to get a PhD."

"I thought you were eighteen."

"I am. I graduated high school early. I've been at MIT since I was fourteen. I finished both my bachelor's and master's in theoretical physics while I was there and then wanted to take a break."

"So, you really are the Monkey King. The lab Monkey King."

"I suppose, but I don't do much practical work in labs."

"So how smart are you?"

"I'm pretty good at some things, like learning, other things I'm not good at all."

"Like what?"

Teddy hadn't been expecting a quiz. He thought for a moment and said, "I know nothing about alpaca farming."

"That doesn't mean you wouldn't be good at it. You could read a book."

"You're right! I would be a great alpaca farmer. What about you?"

"I don't know anything about alpacas."

"I mean, what are your plans after your graphic design degree?"

"I'd like to move to New York and work in advertising or something."

"I hear the Or Something field is booming. I thought you needed grad school for that, though."

Allison laughed. "So, do you have a girlfriend back at MIT?"

"I did, but sadly she was killed by a truck carrying alpacas that jumped the curb while we were walking to a coffee shop."

"See! I would have thought that would have taught you a lesson. It's too bad she dropped the ball as she was training you."

"What do you mean, training?"

Allison smiled and looked at him. "It's the first job we women have when we start dating a guy. We need to fix all their stupid flaws."

"What if he doesn't have anything to fix?"

"All guys have something...perfection can be a flaw, too."

"So deep. I should write that down."

"I really wish you would take notes so I don't have to repeat myself."

A blond guy came up and said, "Hey, Allison."

"Hey."

He was tall and seemed to not even notice Teddy.

"You going out later?"

"I thought I'd stay in and start studying for the new semester."

The guy looked confused. "Really?"

"No. I'm practicing for the regional sarcasm festival at the end of the month. This is my coach, last year's national champion, Teddy."

Now the guy looked impressed. "Wow, that's awesome, dude. I'm Craig, nice to meet you."

Teddy shook his hand.

"Well, I've got to get going. Hope to see you later, Allie. Nice to meet you, Teddy."

Craig walked out, and Teddy asked, "Who was that?"

"That's the rocket scientist I was walking home in shame from last night."

"Damn, I should have checked out his abs."

"They're magnificent."

Teddy wanted to ask more about Craig to find out if she really liked him, but everything he thought to ask sounded really dumb in his head. He sipped his coffee, which was delicious just as the barista had said, and chatted with Allison.

When they had finished, they headed back through the engineering building and up the Ho Chi Minh Trail and were home. Teddy thanked Allison for helping him find his stuff, and she breezed off down the hall.

Teddy watched her walk away. She was really cool.

Billy wasn't around. It was nice since it didn't seem like he had had a moment to himself since he arrived. Teddy put his stuff away and crawled up on his bunk with Hemingway. He read a few more pages but really just wasn't into it. He was into Allison.

The bed was nice. His hangover had subsided, but he was still feeling a bit rundown after his first night of drinking. A nap seemed like a good move.

CHAPTER 31

There were two things that pleased Teddy when he got up at 9:00 a.m. on Monday morning. The first was that he had shown excellent judgment in not scheduling an 8:00 a.m. class. The second was his choice to take a break from physics was a great move.

The practice tailgate party had been a blast. Even a lazy Sunday hanging out in the dorms was more fun than any single day in the last four years at MIT.

His books were in his bag and ready to go. Billy had already left, so Teddy went down to breakfast alone. When he got there, a table of people he had met at the tailgate called him over to eat with them. It was a great start to the day.

The first class was with Dr. Frederick Wellington. Teddy got there fifteen minutes early and picked a seat at the front. The room, trimmed in wood with a triple sliding chalkboard at the front, had a warm feeling. There were pictures of Nabokov, Dickens, Kipling, Proust, Tolstoy, Melville, and Hemingway.

A few more students wandered in, and they were much older than Teddy. Their looks reminded him of his first day at MIT, and Teddy felt small again.

A woman sat down next to Teddy and said, "Dear, this is a graduate course in literature. I think you're in the wrong place." Her tone dripped of condescension.

"That's what people used to say to me when I was at MIT back when I was fourteen. I assure you I'm smart enough to find the right classroom."

She gave him a dirty look and moved to a seat on the other side of the room.

In a flash, the anger and bitterness was back.

The professor walked in with a leather briefcase and set it down on the desk. The chatter quieted. Dr. Wellington went to the chalk board and wrote, The world breaks everyone, and afterward, some are strong at the broken places. He turned around and asked, "Does anyone know who said that?"

Teddy raised his hand a few inches.

Dr. Wellington said, "Yes, you in the front."

"Ernest Hemingway."

"That's correct. What do you think it means?"

"That in his opinion, everyone in the world is weak and gets broken, but those who make it through the trials and tribulations and get up off the mat are stronger for it."

"Why did you say 'in his opinion'?"

"Because the quote is attributed to Mr. Hemingway, thus he is stating his opinion that the entire population of humanity gets broken. I doubt he had evidence to support his position, he is speaking in hyperbole for effect, but nobody would assume it to be a scientifically valid position."

The professor didn't say anything in response to Teddy but just stared at him.

Somebody in the back whispered, "Douche bag."

Teddy didn't raise his hand after that.

His next class wasn't so bad. His mood remained the same. Over half of the class had been in Dr. Wellington's class, too. There were whispers, and Teddy assumed they were about him.

Back at his dorm room, Teddy came in as Billy was heading out. "How was class, Monkey King?"

Teddy shrugged.

"First days always suck. Don't sweat it. I've got a one o'clock, and then I'm going to the gym."

"See you later."

Teddy flopped down on the couch that they had rescued from out front of a house on Sunday. It was strangely comfortable for a garbage couch.

Wigman came by and asked about class, too. Thirty minutes after him, Trish popped in and said, "How was your first class?"

"I think the professor hates me."

"Aw, poor Theodore. Why do you say that?"

"He worships Ernest Hemingway, and he asked me a question, but I didn't give the glowing answer filled with love that he expected of his idol."

"Stand up," she commanded.

Teddy stood.

Trish gave him a long hug. It made him feel better. She smelled nice.

Allison walked in just as the hug was finishing up. "What's going on here?"

Trish said, "Our little Teddy had a rough first day of class. You should give him a hug, too."

Teddy really liked that idea.

Allison said, "Suck it up, Monkey."

Teddy laughed. "How were your classes?"

Trish said, "I've only had one, and it was fine."

Allison said, "I had a lecture class. It was boring."

"You say that about all your classes," Trish joked.

"I blame the administration for not hiring people with personality. Who's going down for lunch?"

"I could eat," Teddy said.

"I was just trying to find Wigman."

"He was just here. I think he was going to go to class and then meet Billy at the gym."

"Thanks," Trish said and gave Teddy another quick hug.

Getting hugs from pretty girls was one of the best spirit lifters Teddy could imagine.

Allison rolled her eyes and said, "Why don't you stick your tongue down his throat? I'm sure that would make him feel better."

Teddy said, "It would, but the pounding from Wigman would probably tip the scales to feeling worse."

Trish stuck her tongue out at Allison and left.

By the time Teddy had finished eating lunch with Allison, he was in a good mood. When Teddy thought about his morning, he was much calmer and decided that he wasn't going to let one professor ruin his new college life.

More people stopped into the room, looking for Billy. Scooter stayed and talked a while. Teddy liked him, he was funny. They played some Xbox baseball, and Teddy only lost 17 – 10. It was the first time he'd got ten runs.

Old habits die hard, and though Teddy didn't have any homework to speak of, he wanted to study. The dorm room wasn't going to be a good place to get some peace and quiet, so he decided to find the library.

Teddy explored the stacks and uncovered a great corner that was almost hidden. Nobody was there, and he picked a comfortable chair to do some reading. If he was required to read Hemingway, he was going to give it his best shot and try to understand why people liked his writing.

CHAPTER 32

The first week was fine. All three of Dr. Wellington's class weren't much fun, but the other classes turned out to be not so bad.

Teddy met with his adviser, Dr. Burns, who shared a similar opinion of both Hemingway and Dr. Wellington, which helped a bunch.

The only bad news was that Allison started dating a wide receiver for the football team. On Saturday, they were out at The Palace, and he and Allison were having a beer when, at just before 1 a.m., the football player asked her if she wanted to dance. She did and never managed to make it back to the table.

It seemed Allison just wasn't around much the next week. Teddy found his mind was preoccupied with what she was up to and how it was going with her new beau.

Sitting in his room with Wigman and Trish, drinking on Friday, he couldn't take it any longer. He had to know. "So, what's Allison been up to?"

Wigman said, "She's been getting pounded by six-foot, three-inch..."

Trish hit Wigman on the shoulder. "Don't be an ass."

"What? She is..."

Trish gave him a look that made Wigman shut up and take a drink of his beer. "She's been spending a lot of time with Trevor."

"I was just curious. He seems nice."

Wigman said, "He's a bit cocky."

Trish said, "Pot...kettle..."

"Whatever."

Teddy said, "Anyone need a beer?"

Two hands went up. Billy came in with Allison. "Look who I found!"

Wigman said, "Teddy boy has been missing you."

Teddy got a little red. "I was just asking..."

Allison said, "Ah, you've missed me, Monkey. I'm touched."

Billy said, "It's Monkey King."

"Whatever."

Teddy got beers out of the minifridge and made sure everyone was covered. Those beers led to another round and then another before Wigman pointed out that they were getting low.

Trish offered to go buy more, and she took Allison with her.

As soon as they were gone, Wigman said, "So, you got a thing for Allison?"

Billy said, "Who doesn't? She's smoking hot and can drink like a Russian sailor on shore leave."

Teddy said, "You like Allison?"

"Nah, I'm just saying, she's great. Why wouldn't you want to throw her down and give her the royal treatment?"

"You think she's out of my league?"

Wigman said, "Hell yes!"

Teddy looked deflated.

"You don't think Trish is out of my league? She's smarter than me, way better looking, and is a much better person in general. Did that stop me?"

Billy said, "You should have seen Wigman last year. He had it bad for Trish, and she was dating a wrestler."

"What did you do?"

"I stayed close. I knew the guy she was with would screw up."

Billy said, "Oh, did he screw up. Trish was planning on going home one weekend, and her car broke down about two hundred miles from here. She ended up having to come back to campus."

Teddy opened one of the remaining four beers and said, "What happened?"

"She had a key to his apartment and walked in to find one of the mat aides giving him a..."

"She walked in on it, wow, she must have been pissed."

"She threw his PlayStation into his TV and destroyed both of them."

"What did you do?"

"I swooped in to pick up the pieces."

"What do you mean?"

Billy said, "He didn't swoop at all. He spent an entire Friday night in her dorm room, listening to her cry. Wigman didn't close the deal for another week."

Teddy said, "That was pretty classy that you didn't take advantage of her."

"If I'm honest, I tried a couple of times, but she shut me down."

Billy laughed. "I have to give him credit, he was patient and got her in the end."

Teddy didn't get the crude double entendre or understand why Wigman and Billy high-fived. He didn't care, it gave him hope. "You think I have a chance then?"

Wigman said, "Fuck no."

Teddy grinned.

"I'm just kidding. You just need to play your cards right."

"I don't really know anything about women."

"Nobody does."

Billy said, "We've got your back, Monkey King. Wigman and I can teach you everything you need to know."

Wigman said, "Yes! Team Teddy. I'll do recon when I'm with Trish and keep tabs on her and Trevor."

Billy said, "You need to just be a good friend, but not too good a friend."

"What do you mean?"

"The friend zone is inescapable."

"How do I know if I'm being too good a friend?"

"You can't always be available for her. She'll think you're a pussy."

"I don't understand."

"Okay, you need to develop a routine where you two hang out. Maybe have lunch every Tuesday, but after three or four lunches, you cancel."

"Why?"

"She'll start to miss you."

Wigman said, "You should make her jealous, too."

"Are you kidding? She's dating a football player, how could I possibly make her jealous?"

"Don't you worry about it, you can."

Billy said, "Oh, and when you two are talking, try to mimic her body movements."

Teddy was getting more confused by the minute.

Wigman said, "Like this," he had Billy stand up. Billy flipped his hair and said, "Oh my gawd, did you see the last episode of Jersey Shore?"

Teddy said, "She watches Jersey Shore?"

Wigman said, "Shush, not the point."

Billy said, "It was amazing."

Wigman moved his body to keep it parallel with Billy's and nodded at everything she said. "See what I'm doing? I'm pretending to listen and keeping our bodies sort of linked."

"What does that do?"

Billy said, "It's subtle, and it makes them feel connected."

Wigman said, "If she touches her hair, that's a good sign."

"You've got to be kidding."

"No, this shit's real, dude."

Teddy said, "I'll be back. This beer is going through me like...beer."

In the hall, the sounds of youth banged off the walls. Music, laughter, and video game gunfire floated out from the rooms. Two pretty girls hung out in the doorway of a room. They smiled at Teddy as he walked past. He gave them a nod.

The buzz of the beers was something, the high of having friends was even better. But what he really wanted was Allison. She was living in his mind twenty-four/seven. He wondered if this was normal. It certainly didn't seem like it.

CHAPTER 33

Teddy thought about the advice he'd been given a lot that weekend...all the way up to the point he stepped into Dr. Wellington's class. It was the first time he had not beaten the professor to class.

He stood like a sentinel at the chalkboard with the papers they had turned in on Friday. The other students filed in and took their seats. At precisely 10:00 a.m., Dr. Wellington said, "I'm returning your papers. They were all rubbish. I expect rewrites on Friday."

He walked from desk to desk and dropped each paper like it was infested with the plague. Teddy looked at his paper, and the only mark on it was a red letter F.

The groans from the other students told the story. Teddy snuck a look at the guy sitting two chairs down, he had an F also.

Teddy was in shock. He'd never even got a B before, and this was unthinkable. He flipped through the pages, looking for the mistakes. There wasn't a single red mark other than the horrible letter at the top righthand corner of page one.

Dr. Wellington began his lecture. "We must not only learn to read the great works, we must be able to write on their level. One would not describe Tchaikovsky as a cool dude, and you will not be permitted to insult literary giants with your poorly thought-out essays."

Teddy raised his hand and asked, "What are some of the conclusions in the papers that you found objectionable?"

"I didn't read any of your first drafts, I never do. It is impossible to get something right without multiple revisions. Hemingway used to do dozens of drafts before he was done."

A few of the students nodded in agreement, while a couple of others made audible noises of disgust. Teddy sat stunned.

He had been judged a failure based solely on the ineptitude of a long-dead, and horrible, writer.

The professor droned on, and Teddy ignored him. The shock wore off and slowly turned to anger.

After class, Teddy was spitting mad. His adviser's office wasn't far. The secretary said he wasn't in, but a grumbling noise said otherwise. The door opened, and Dr. Burns said, "This student I like. I'm always in for Theodore."

"Thanks, Dr. Burns."

"You look miffed," he said and pointed to a chair.

Teddy took out his paper and put it on the desk. "Dr. Wellington told the entire class he didn't even read it!"

"Yes, I've heard he does that. You must remember that at his best, he is a failed writer who has devoted the last forty years to taking out his frustration over his crushed dreams on his students."

"What is he at his worst?"

"Ernest Hemingway."

Teddy chuckled a little. "Why does he like Hemingway so much? I just don't get it. I can't find anything even remotely interesting by Hemingway. The Old Man and the Sea was okay, but it wasn't genius."

"I agree, but the question is why?"

"I don't know. It just didn't do anything for me."

"That's not much of an answer."

Teddy thought for a while and then said, "You're right, it isn't."

"I'm not one to give advice, especially to my advisees, but you're not like most of the spoiled dregs of society who are sent off to campus as a condition of their trust funds. I suspect you're looking for something of value, almost spiritual, here at Beckerston, you're not just here to get laid."

"I'd like to get laid, too."

Dr. Burns grinned and continued, "Literature, like everything, can be uplifting, it can be genius, it can inspire, but it is also easily corrupted."

"What do you mean, corrupted?"

"Imagine a small-time artist catches the fancy of a wealthy collector. She buys a couple of pieces and hangs them on her wall. It's pure. One day, she decides it would be great if everyone loved the artist as much as she does. She starts to talk him up among her society friends and builds up a fan base before most of them have even seen the work.

"She wants to own an original Chagall but can't afford one, so she's going to make her own Chagall.

"Writers can be the same. Everyone wants to be a king maker, especially those who lack the artistic skill they so admire. Most people are stupid, but some of those idiots are great at inheriting millions and they need something to do.

"Teddy, I think you would be well served to find out the why you don't find Hemingway to be a genius or more importantly, why others do."

"If there is one thing I can do...it's research. Thanks, Dr. Burns."

"Well then, my work here is done. Get out of here so I can continue my nap."

Teddy's mood was lifted. He went to his next class and then to the library. He was going to get to know Hemingway beyond just his words. The answer was somewhere in the stacks.

* * *

Ernest Hemingway wrote letters his whole life, and Teddy discovered a volume dedicated to his correspondence. It was hard to concentrate for some reason. He'd read a little, and his mind would wander.

There was something about the dates, the intimacy, the people's names after "Dear", that made Teddy want to meet them. He was sure that Hemingway's friends would know why his writing was so loved.

Teddy didn't know that Hemingway had worked at the Kansas City Star for six months as a journalist. It was in 1917, and he scribbled it into his notebook. It lasted for six months until May of 1918 when Hemingway decided to head to New York.

He liked fishing and the lakes of northern Michigan. Teddy had never been fishing. He wasn't sure why it was fun, but many people did it so there must be a reason.

Before he'd even finished the introduction, Teddy found something he really liked. Hemingway often corresponded with some literary giants he admired such as T.S. Eliot, Robert Frost, Gertrude Stein, Ezra Pound, and James Joyce, though Teddy had to admit he wasn't a huge fan of Joyce. Still, it made sense that Hemingway would know them.

The temptation was to flip to the letters between Hemingway and the other authors, but he resisted. Teddy read on and then found a gem. Ernest Hemingway's chief rival of the age was Faulkner. Teddy loved William Faulkner, and learning about the relationship with Hemingway gave him a sense of choosing sides. He was in the Faulkner camp.

His phone buzzed with a text message. It was from Allison, "You busy?"

"Not really, what's up?"

"Edgar's?"

"Sure, when?"

"I'm almost there now."

"L8R," Teddy texted back. He didn't like most text shorthand and preferred to use proper grammar and punctuation, but something about the clever use of a number resonated.

Teddy checked out his book and headed for the bar. Allison was at a booth when he got there. "I got us a pitcher."

"Early afternoon drinking on a Monday?"

"Don't be a pussy."

Teddy poured a glass. "How was your day?"

"Trevor's an idiot."

"How so?"

"He texted me and said he'd talked to my father."

"Why is that so strange?"

"My dad passed away when I was twelve."

"Oh, I'm sorry."

"Thanks, but that's not the point. He knows my father is dead."

"Is it some sort of sick joke?"

"No, he thought he was texting his ex."

"Well, that's not good."

"You're damn right it's not good. What an ass."

Teddy was trying to remember the advice Billy and Wigman had given him, but she was just sitting there, so there wasn't much he could do. He had no idea what he should say about Trevor.

On one hand, he could agree with her and call him an ass; on the other, he could try to point out that it was a rather harmless text. Teddy was sure there was a best move, but he had no idea which one was it. He decided to error on the side of reason.

Teddy said, "I'm sure he didn't mean anything by it. He was just passing on a message that he'd spoken to her father. Perhaps they were close?"

"I don't give a rat's ass about him talking with her father. What I want to know is why he's texting her at all."

225

It was obvious Teddy had chosen poorly. He decided to retreat. "You're right, he's just begging her to come over and jump into his bed...if you read between the lines. Were there multiple lines?"

"You joke, but how do I know they're not still hooking up?"

"How serious are you about this guy?"

"He's my boyfriend; what do you think?"

"I have no idea. I've only known you for a few weeks. Do you love him?"

"No, of course not, but that's not the point."

Teddy was confident he had no idea what the point was, but thought it best to play along. "I know. So, what are you going to do about it?"

Allison finished off her beer and poured another. "How was your day?"

"My professor is a dick."

"Really, what did he do?"

Teddy took out the paper to show her. "I've never got less than an A. And now I have an F. He told the class that he didn't even read them."

"That is a total dick move, but he's letting you rewrite it, right?"

"I don't want to rewrite it. I spent a lot of time to get it just right the first time...like I always do."

"So, you're just going to take the F?"

"No, probably not."

"Rewrite it, then."

"I hate him. He's got this obsession with Hemingway."

"What's wrong with that?"

"Are you kidding me? Have you read A Farewell to Arms?"

"I read The Old Man and the Sea in high school. It wasn't so bad."

"Okay, I'll admit it was fair, but his other stuff is just so bland. It's like a Dick and Jane book."

"A what?"

"Never mind."

"You're really worked up, Monkey King."

"I know."

"What are you going to do?"

Teddy looked at his beer and pounded it.

Allison poured him another one. "That was my plan for Trevor."

"If we drink enough, will it solve our problems?"

"History shows that it won't, but I'm willing to give it a try anyway."

They finished the pitcher and got another. He loved getting to just hang out with her. She was quick witted and beautiful. It was an amazing combination. Being a Monday, the Pit was mostly empty throughout the afternoon. At around nine o'clock, people started to pile in, and he and Allison were well on their way to really smashed.

She had moved over to his side of the booth. It was intoxicating being so close to her. They slowed up the drinking around ten but kept hanging out and telling stories. He learned about her years at camp when she was young, the first boy she'd ever kissed, and the name of every one of her pets.

Teddy told her the story about how he had helped the FBI, and she seemed impressed. At some point, she was touching her leg to his. Was she doing it on purpose? Did it mean anything? What should I do?

They left the bar at one in the morning. Allison walked slowly and took Teddy's hand. She locked fingers with him, and they didn't talk much. A breeze, slight but warm, blew the clouds away, and the stars peeked through.

The bench was situated between two oak trees, and they sat there for a while. Teddy's head was in a haze. Everything seemed perfect. I should kiss her, he thought, but then his voice said, but it's perfect now. Teddy wished he'd got more notes from Billy and Wigman. He wasn't ready for the bench.

"What a beautiful night," Allison said.

"It's perfect."

"I just wish..."

There was a long silence, and they both seemed to be dying to find out what she was going to say next. It hung there while the world spun around.

Allison tried again. "I just wish I...what I mean..."

Teddy squeezed her hand. She laid her head on his shoulder and said, "I think Trish is staying with Wigman."

Teddy stood up and lifted Allison to her feet. The dorms were about four blocks away, and nothing needed to be said.

Hilltop was still up, there were a few parties going, and those with fake IDs were making their way back from the bars. Teddy had his arm around her shoulder when they got to her room. A note was taped to the door. It was from Trevor.

The spell was broken.

CHAPTER 34

Teddy threw himself into researching Hemingway. It took his mind off Allison. It seemed that Trevor had apologized profusely and the next day bought her flowers. All was forgiven.

When he wasn't in the library, Teddy had started hanging out with Scooter. Scooter loved playing pool, and Teddy had wanted to learn. It was a game full of physics, and Teddy took to it like a duck to a Disney film.

The Palace had a nice table in back. Teddy would put up quarters when they arrived. Usually, there were four or five games in front of them. When he and Scooter got to the table, they made quick work of the fraternity boys and set to defending the table. The first night, they played together they held it for five hours.

Teddy had never been good at any sort of competition unrelated to academics, and this was a blast. Scooter was quite the trash talker, too.

He would get in people's heads, and they'd miss shots because they weren't concentrating. That was as big a part of his game as cue ball control. One Thursday night, Teddy and Scooter had been on the table for a few hours and the bar had just given last call. There was time for one more game.

Most of the time, they played for fun, but the guys from the SAE house were having an especially hard time dealing with the butt kicking. They had insisted on betting ten dollars a game. Down thirty, one of the guys who Teddy thought looked like a Chet, said, "One more game," and he slapped a hundred down on the table.

Scooter, who was sporting a hat that looked it was straight out of The Maltese Falcon, pulled out five twenties and laid them on top of the hundred. "My boy Teddy's got this break."

People had started to watch a few games earlier, and now there was quite a crowd. Half the baseball team was there and watching as Teddy chalked his cue.

Scooter stood next to him and whispered, "You remember that break I showed you? Second ball on the right, back left spin on the cue ball, and give it a solid whack."

The music faded out. It was almost closing time. Teddy gave the cue a bit more chalk, set the chalk down, and gave it a crack.

The balls exploded apart. The little white ball caromed off the rack and went straight into the side rail and back toward the rack. The guys from SAE and their fraternity brothers watched a couple balls fall in the corner.

Scooter reached down and swiped up the money with one hand and tipped his hat with the other. "Thanks, boys."

"What?" said Chet.

The cue ball had struck the eight and was sending it slowly toward the side pocket. It was moving just slowly enough that Chet saw what was happening. Teddy watched in amazement and when the eight fell, the crowd exploded.

The baseball team, their girlfriends, and others who had been watching, mobbed Teddy. Scooter yelled, "After hours at my place...compliments of SAE."

It was the pool shot heard round campus. It seemed like everyone had been there, everyone except Allison.

Trish had seen it, though, and Teddy was sure she'd tell her roommate.

That Sunday, Scooter took Teddy to the student union to practice. About an hour into knocking balls around the table, Scooter said, "I need a favor, Teddy."

"Sure."

"I've got a test coming up, and I need to pass it, or I'll lose my eligibility for baseball and my scholarship."

"What's the subject?"

"Math."

"I'm excellent at math."

"I know, that's why I asked."

"You came to the right place."

"So you'll do it?"

"Sure...wait...what?"

"You'll take the test for me."

"You want me to take your test, are you kidding?"

"Come on, you've got to help me. If I lose my scholarship, my dad will kill me."

"If I help you cheat and we get caught, I can kiss my PhD in physics goodbye and the rest of my career."

"We won't get caught, I promise."

Teddy didn't say anything. He liked Scooter.

Scooter started to get mad. "Listen, Teddy, you've got to help me. You don't dawg the boys, and if you don't, you'll not only be screwing me, but the whole team. You want to make enemies of everyone?"

Scooter was much bigger than Teddy and more than a little bit scary, but Teddy had been here before.

"The last time somebody tried to bully me into helping them, I agreed. Do you know what happened?"

"No."

"I had this group of friends when I was in high school, or I thought they were my friends. It turns out they just liked me because I'm a genius and could hack things they couldn't. They wanted to rob Citibank. They were just like you, threatening me, and I was only thirteen at the time. It sucked.""

"This isn't the same as..."

"Shut up, and listen. I agreed to help them. I knew it was wrong, and so I set them up. I went to the FBI and helped the feds get every last one of those jerks who pretended to be my friend. Let me ask you a question."

"You ratted them out?"

"One of them got thirty years. Will you answer one question for me?"

"What?"

"How important is baseball to you?"

"It means everything."

"You've probably been dreaming about it since you were a little kid."

"Since I was four years old and first started hitting off a tee in the back yard with my dad, so yes."

"You work hard at it, right?"

"I'm the hardest working guy on the team. I never miss a workout or weight session."

"If the coach said run an extra mile…"

"I'd run two."

"So you'd be willing to do anything to play the game you love?"

"Yes, anything, that's why I came to you…I need your help."

"Did you mean it, you'd do anything?"

"Yes, what do you want, cash?"

"I love physics as much as you do baseball. I've been working toward a career in theoretical physics for as long as I can remember. Academic dishonesty is a one-strike game. One time, and I'm done forever, my dream of winning a Nobel Prize is no more. Do you really want to ask me to risk so much?"

"But we won't get caught," Scooter said deflated.

"You said you'd do anything."

"Yes!"

"Will you let me teach you what you need to pass?"

"I can't do math. It's algebra, and there aren't any numbers. It's all those damned letters."

"Do you know how to calculate batting average?"

"Yes, but that's different."

"Do you know your batting average the last two years?"

"Yes, but I still don't…"

"What's 17 percent of 350?"

"I have no idea, and I don't see…"

"What's 17 percent of one hundred?"

"Seventeen," he said with a "duh" voice.

"Can you tell me what seventeen times three equals?"

Scooter thought about it for a moment and answered, "Fifty-one."

"Right. Can you tell me what half of seventeen equals?"

"Eight and a half."

"What's fifty-one plus eight and a half?"

"Fifty nine and a half."

"So, you did know what 17 percent of 350 was, you just didn't know you knew it."

Scooter didn't say anything for a little bit. He started to say something, but stopped, then said, "That wasn't really a fair test because you were asking me all the right questions."

"All I have to do before your test is teach you the right questions."

Scooter stuck out his hand and said, "Deal."

* * *

It took less than three hours for the light to go on over Scooter's head. He was sharp, but every time the subject of math came up he stressed out to the point where he couldn't think. They peeled back the layers that had shrouded math in mystery, and when Scooter came out the other side, he finally got it.

He scored an eighty-five on his test, which was so much better than he had ever got before he made Teddy go with him to talk to the professor and explain how he had suddenly got so good at math.

There was some skepticism, but Teddy walked him through how they had turned the corner with Scooter.

From that day forward, math was Scooter's favorite subject.

Teddy even got a call from the manager of the baseball team, thanking him for keeping his star shortstop eligible.

It was a good win for all.

Dr. Wellington's class, however, remained a thorn in Teddy's side. The tests were fine, as all he needed to do was recount the points spewed out during lectures. Teddy could do that all day long, but the papers, they were nearly impossible. It wasn't good enough to make a reasonable argument, one needed to make a strong case for why Dr. Wellington was right.

It was unbearable. Teddy was convinced he was the worst professor to ever enter a classroom. He was becoming obsessed. Lying on his bed while Billy played Xbox, he said, "It's like he's intentionally being obtuse."

"I don't know what that means, but did you see that zombie's head explode?"

"He refuses to accept any other opinions other than his own. Even William Faulkner said of Hemingway, 'He has never been known to use a word that might send a reader to the dictionary.'"

Billy fired off a rocket launcher and said, "I hate looking words up in the dictionary. I usually just skip the ones I don't know."

"Check out what Vladimir Nabokov said, 'As to Hemingway, I read him for the first time in the early 'forties, something about bells, balls and bulls, and loathed it.'"

"I like hockey."

"What?"

"Isn't Nabokov a forward for the Washington Capitals?"

"No, he wrote Lolita, which was a New York Times Best Seller in 1959."

"Then I've never heard of him."

"You're missing the point."

Billy was in a tough spot with a horde of small pinkish creatures with horrible-looking fangs and had stopped listening all together.

Teddy jumped off the bunk and grabbed his back pack. It didn't matter that Billy didn't want to listen to him ramble on about Hemingway, as killing and mayhem was way more fun. Teddy understood and didn't mind.

What did matter was his grade, which currently stood at a B. An unfathomable position not so long ago, but Teddy wasn't going to let Dr. Wellington defeat him. The final paper was worth 40 percent of the grade, and Teddy could choose to write about anything he wanted.

The union was a great place to study. Teddy would often hang out in the afternoon between classes and read.

Today, there were a couple of tables where people were playing speed chess in the main common area. Normally, he would have sat down and watched or even played a few games, but not today. Teddy was in no mood.

He had been searching for the core reason behind his hatred of Hemingway. It wasn't just that the writing was insultingly simplistic or boring, there was something else.

The letters Hemingway wrote were stylistically the same as his writing. They were without cadence or harmony, they lacked the music that Teddy believed flowed beneath any truly great piece of prose. Never had Teddy set down a book by Ernest Hemingway because of a passage so beautifully crafted that it needed to be savored and considered before moving on.

Teddy wrote down the word slow in his notes. It was another mark against Dr. Wellington's favorite writer. It took forever for Hemingway to make a point. Even diehard fans of Hemingway hated his Across the River and into the Trees.

Teddy couldn't understand, despite every effort, how anyone with a modicum of intelligence could think Hemingway was brilliant. He looked into the history of The Old Man and the Sea because it was the one book Teddy didn't mind. He didn't love it, but that novella wasn't a waste of time like his novels.

He flipped back to his notes on The Old Man and the Sea. It was published through Life Magazine in 1952. Teddy knew how popular Life had been back then. It could be found on the coffee tables of families all across the country. It made sense that people would have read it, and if they enjoyed it (because they had heard of Hemingway and knew he was a famous literary writer), that they might feel smarter themselves for understanding the work.

This must surely explain how The Old Man and the Sea won the Pulitzer Prize in 1953 and then the Nobel in Literature in 1954, but it didn't. Those prizes weren't based upon popularity, they were judged by people who abhorred anything the masses might enjoy.

Teddy had always believed that those who judged writing for a living were simply people who couldn't do something important. They were the dullards of society who chose the worst possible tomes to elevate, knowing that John Q. Public wouldn't like them. These literati could then claim that the work was simply above their heads, and thus ascribe a level of intelligence to themselves that they couldn't get through real critical thinking.

These theories were diametrically opposed. Hemingway was loved by the masses, who, by definition, were of average intelligence, and the literary gatekeepers, who were, in Teddy's estimation, of below-average intelligence.

The clack of the chess pieces and the thwack of hands hitting clocks was the perfect white noise for Teddy to think. He didn't notice some of his classmates from Dr. Wellington's class had sat down one table over until one of them said, "Look who it is, Sky, Teddy Alexander."

The tone had an unmistakable sneer to it. Teddy only knew their names because the professor had called on them. He hadn't actually talked to his classmates. He looked over and gave a nod and then went back to his notes.

Sky said, "Why don't you drop the class? Nobody likes you, and you don't seem to 'get' literature."

Teddy was still in a foul mood. He turned and said, "I'm here because I love literature. I'm taking a couple of years off from my career just to dig deeper and get to the soul of the great works. Why are you here? Is it because you have no choice?"

"I have plenty of choices. I was an art major before..."

"I mean choices that matter."

"You don't think art matters?"

"I love art, I love books, but that isn't a career...unless you're unable to do something important."

Sky and the others howled and cussed at Teddy. They called him all sorts of names, and Teddy didn't care.

Sky said, "What did physics ever do for mankind?"

Teddy looked incredulous and said, "Your stupidity is staggering. I could spend the next twenty years explaining why physics, along with the other sciences, has created the society we enjoy today, but..."

A guy named Marc said, "Today's society is nothing but greedy capitalists."

Teddy shot back, "Why do you think Hemingway is a genius?"

Marc said, "He's one of the great writers of..."

"I said why, do you think you could stick to the question?"

"He won a Pulitzer and a Nobel Prize."

"Yes he did, but why?"

Marc said, "Percy Hutchinson said in a review for the New York Times of A Farewell To Arms, 'It was a moving and beautiful book,' and I would agree."

"So, do you have any original thoughts? No, of course you don't. Why did YOU like it?"

The challenge was too much for Marc to meet.

Teddy continued, "I can tell you why I didn't like it. Hemingway portrays the love interest, Catherine, as a mindless lovesick paper doll with no personality and zero sense of value except that which she receives through the eyes of her man, Henry. She is dull, the prototypical future housewife whose only purpose in life is to have babies for her man."

Teddy looked at Sky and said, "Why doesn't his portrayal of Catherine offend your feminist sensibilities?"

Sky had nothing.

Teddy was on a roll. He tore through The Sun Also Rises with equal vitriol, and when he was done his classmates made a few remarks about his age and not belonging and then left. Teddy remained livid. They were truly mindless drones looking for the path of least resistance in academia in the hopes they could join people like Dr. Wellington and share in the wonders of tenure and elitism.

The trip to the union hadn't helped his mood. It had been a complete waste of time...or had it? He walked toward Edgar's Pit, where he was sure a burger basket would help his terrible mood, and a seed of insight seemed to have been planted. He may have accidentally got to the core of not only his dislike of Hemingway but also Dr. Wellington.

Edgar's Pit wasn't very full. Teddy went to the bar and ordered a burger basket. A voice from behind him said, "Hey, Teddy."

He turned around and it was Allison sitting at a table with Trevor. Teddy mustered a weak, "Hey," and turned back to the bartender and said, "I'll be in the back."

Teddy headed for the back room, which was dark, had several nice alcoves where one could talk, or in this case, think, and it was as far as possible from Allison and Trevor.

240

Teddy pretended he didn't hear her when for him to join then. His mood had got worse.

He opened his notebook and took out two pens. There were a million thoughts running through his head, but they were all too blurry to figure out. It was as if Hemingway and Allison were battling in his brain, and the war that raged for his attention made all reasonable thought impossible.

He noticed Allison heading his direction. Teddy made it a point to hover over his notes and assume a position of epic concentration. She continued past on the way to the women's restroom.

Teddy really didn't want to talk to her right now.

A few minutes later, she was standing by his alcove, arms crossed. "What's your problem?"

"I'm busy."

"I'm not leaving until you tell me what's crawled up your butt."

"You don't want that."

"I'm serious, what the fuck have I done to you?"

Teddy stood. "You want to know what my problem is?"

"Yes."

"It's you...and...Trevor. Are you kidding me? Why are you with him? He's an idiot and..."

"He's not an idiot."

"Yes he is, he's not going to ever play professional football, because he's the third option on a Division III team. He's studying communications, and he can barely string together a coherent sentence."

"I think you're..."

241

"He's not going to be able to be a broadcaster because NOBODY says, "Um, you know" between every independent clause unless they're a professional athlete being interviewed by someone who speaks well, and as I've just said, he's never going to go pro."

"That's not fair, I think..."

"You're not thinking at all, you just like dating a football player. In another year, he's going to have graduated and will be working as a garbage man or working for a landscape architecture company, making minimum wage to mow successful people's lawns."

"Now you're just being mean."

"I'm being honest. You two have no future, and you know it."

"Where is all of this coming from?"

Teddy glared at her and said, "Because you belong with me." He grabbed her and gave her a kiss right on the mouth. It was a hard, aggressive kiss. He grabbed her around the waist and pulled her into him.

The bartender arrived with the burger basket and set it down just as Teddy pulled away. He looked at the bartender, pulled out his wallet, and gave her a twenty. With a swipe of his arm he slid his stuff into his backpack and said, "Thanks for the burger, but I've lost my appetite." Teddy didn't even look back as he left.

Allison said, "Wait, Teddy."

Teddy was halfway down the block when she caught him. She grabbed his arm and said, "Wait, we need to talk."

Teddy kept walking. "No, we don't."

Allison caught him again and grabbed his face. She got right up on him until their noses were almost touch-

ing. "You're right, he is an idiot." S
properly, and the anger over everythi
a long kiss, the type that stays with a
his life.

When it was done, she said, "Le.
or comes out. He may be stupid, but he's still freaking
huge."

Teddy took her hand, and they ran. He had the girl,
and if she didn't mind a cowardly retreat, then who was
he to argue?

They went back to Teddy's room. Billy and Wigman
were in an epic baseball battle on the Xbox. Teddy said,
"Get out."

Billy and Wigman looked up, saw Teddy holding
hands with Allison, who had a little bit of a blush in her
cheeks. Billy hit the power button, and without a word
he and Wigman left.

There's a Latin proverb that says, "Fortune favors
the bold," and an hour ago it had meant nothing to Teddy. He had spent his entire life afraid of nothing, except
girls. His mind was too quick to figure out reasons he
would fail than to simply go for it. The fear of rejection
was too powerful to overcome, but from somewhere
deep inside of him, a boldness had bubbled forth, and
he had won the day.

That first night with Allison would be counted
among his most cherished memories, better than getting his bachelor's degree or graduating top of his class
in his master's program. It was the moment he found
something in himself he didn't know existed.

From that point forward, Teddy had a girlfriend, and more importantly, he had a trusted ear. It was the latter that he most needed.

CHAPTER 35

Teddy was dreading going to class and seeing Sky, Marc, and the others, but he wasn't going to skip just because it would be uncomfortable. As it turned out, both Marc and Sky skipped that day, and the other two didn't say a word to Teddy.

A teaching assistant announced that Dr. Wellington wasn't able to make it to class and she would be continuing their discussion on Proust. The TA had a refreshing energy about her, and the lecture was much more interesting because of it.

In the time between classes, Teddy went to the student union to do some more reading of Hemingway's letters, but he really just wanted to see Allison. The book sat open and ignored as he thought about the state of their union.

Since he first started crushing on Karen in high school, Teddy had spent countless hours trying to figure out how to get a girlfriend and a fair amount of time wondering what he would do if he succeeded. There had always been a lingering fear of success. For as little as he knew about understanding women, he knew less about how to make them happy as a boyfriend.

The most amazing thing happened when they woke up together, all the crushing fears Teddy had expected to ambush him and mess with his mind, didn't show up. The insecurity about dating that had haunted him simply disappeared when he looked her in the eyes and confessed.

Allison had opened her eyes, given him a smile, and said, "Don't kiss me, my morning breath could kill a rhino."

Teddy had covered his own mouth and laughed. "I need to confess something, too."

"Go for it."

"I understand there are a lot of rules. I've heard it's a mistake if I call you in the next two days. I need to pretend I don't like you that much. And a good boyfriend should never lie to his girl."

She just listened with a look that Teddy couldn't really describe, but he absolutely adored. He wanted to just grab her and kiss her rhino breath and all. He didn't; he had more to say.

"Here's the problem. I don't want to lie to you, but if I pretend I don't like you that much, well, then that would be a lie. I also don't like the two-day rule."

"So, what you're saying is you want to be my boyfriend, starting immediately, and you're asking for a waiver of the two-day, no-call rule."

Teddy couldn't help but chuckle at her legalese-sounding response. "Yes, your honor."

"Having reviewed your record since last night, I'm granting you a boyfriendship and waving the no-call rule. As for not lying to me, that's a tricky area. The law is clear that a boyfriend is technically never supposed to lie to his girl, but if said girl asks if an outfit makes her look fat, and it does, then honest is NOT the best policy. So, I'm afraid you're on your own on that one."

Teddy's chuckles to himself went unnoticed by the folks at the union. He had a girlfriend, and more importantly, he had one who made being a boyfriend easy.

Teddy went back to the book. He read with notebook at his side, looking for more arguments to strengthen his case that Hemingway was a fraud, a charlatan of the first order, and should be hated by all. Then something horrible happened, he read a passage that he could neither dislike, nor could he disagree with it.

The passage mentioned Hemingway's competitive spirit and a disgust of sloppy workmanship. Teddy loved competing, especially in academia, and he also hated people who couldn't be bothered to do their work well. Teddy didn't want to like these traits, but he knew it was dishonest to discount them, so he noted them and moved on.

There was mention of Hemingway's desire to avoid imitation, which Teddy also admired, even if he found the end result to be less appealing than taking a tour of a slaughterhouse. Original thought was to be admired as an achievement unto itself. Teddy wrote this down, too.

Just before any sort of fondness could take hold of Teddy, he ran across a letter to Dorothy Connable dated 16 February 1920, in which Hemingway is giving advice on how to win at roulette.

He begins by explaining to his friend that the odds are stacked in the house's favor because they only pay out thirty-six to one on a chance of thirty-eight to one, but then he does the unthinkable, he suggests a martingale betting strategy as a way to profit at roulette. Hemingway suggests his friend watch which numbers haven't come up in a while and then choose them for the wager. If the bet loses, then double it the next time.

Teddy was almost too angry to write. A hand on his shoulder broke the spell.

"Hey there, Monkey, what's up?"

"Listen to this," Teddy said, and then read the letter to Allison, who had sat down next to him. A five-minute explanation of why this was the stupidest thing ever uttered by a human being followed.

Allison listened, and before Teddy could burst into flames she leaned over and gave him little kiss and said, "You're so cute when you go on a math rant."

It was technically a statistics rant, but Teddy didn't think correcting her would win him more kisses, so he let it slide. "I think I need a Danish, how about you?"

"Cream cheese, please."

CHAPTER 36

Over the remainder of the fall semester, Dr. Wellington only managed to attend two of the classes, and he was in a terrible mood both times. Teddy couldn't help but argue with him because it seemed the professor was incapable of logical thought. Teddy's mood soured after each exchange.

Tuesday of finals week arrived, and the paper was finally finished. He would hand it in on Wednesday but not before getting Allison's thoughts.

They sat at their favorite booth in Edgar's Pit, and Teddy read, "And in conclusion, the entire body of work was propped up by the journalists, editors, and New York publishing machine that adored the man and had the power to make anyone a star. Ernest Hemingway was not a genius. He was, at best, the literary equivalent of a boy band propped up by the adoration of masses of intellectually bankrupt sycophants. He was a fraud."

Allison took a sip of her beer.

"What do you think?"

There was some hesitation. Teddy saw it in her eyes.

"Don't tell me you like it because you like me."

"You make a strong and reasoned argument."

Teddy took a sip of his beer, the "But?" was implied. Somebody played "Wonderful World" by Louis Armstrong.

Allison said, "I love this song."

"I do, too. You can finish your thoughts on my paper. I can take it."

"Just listen to the song," she said, taking his hand.

* * *

The office was quiet. Dr. Wellington's secretary greeted Teddy and then said, "You may leave your paper with me."

"I'd prefer to hand it in personally, if that's okay."

"Dr. Wellington isn't seeing..."

A tired voice from behind the closed office door said, "Send him in, Ruth."

Ruth looked sad but nodded to the door.

Teddy opened the door and walked in. Dr. Wellington was sitting in his chair, staring out the window. A picture of his wife rested in his lap. A file folder that didn't look like the type used by most professors at Beckerston sat on the desk, closed.

"You can leave your paper on the desk, Mr. Alexander. I'm sure it will be insightful."

Sorrow hung in the air. Teddy's hand clutched the report and couldn't seem to set it down. "I think...what I mean is...on the walk over I realized that one more rewrite was probably in order. I'll get it to you by the end of the day."

"That will be fine."

Teddy left the office, unsure why he'd just said that. He went to the library and made his way back to his favorite spot. Worn-out looking students were scattered all about in the hopes of packing one more tiny bit of learning into their brains before finals.

He didn't have any ideas about what he might change. A copy of the day's student newspaper was on the table behind him, and he grabbed it. Just below the fold was a small mention of Dr. Wellington's wife, who had passed away after a six-week battle with stage-four cancer.

Teddy opened his laptop and made a copy of his paper. It was almost twice as long as required, he read and cut, then added a little here and there. He added a few bits to take the edge off of his criticism. He made it to the ending and reread it twice before deleting the section.

He began to type, "Literature, at its core, teaches us something about ourselves. There is always a lesson to be learned, and it differs for each person who turns the pages. We all view the prose through our own lens and see the world as we want it to be, not as it is, or as the author intended.

"I don't like his style and find his storytelling leaves me cold, but that's because I had never truly looked at the man and his words, for they cannot be separated without lessening the truth hidden within.

"Ernest Hemingway was a complex man who crafted tales that spoke to millions. For every argument made against his work, there are others who defend his writing with equal passion. Louis Armstrong once said of

251

music, 'If it sounds good, it is good.' My dislike of Hemingway doesn't change the indisputable fact he spoke to many who think he's an excellent writer.

"What is the value in changing another person's mind?

"Perhaps there is more value in looking inward and asking why I need to have others agree with me. It doesn't change the words, it won't take back the enjoyment others have found, and that's a good thing.

"It's better to realize that any man who has managed to use his typewriter to give so many people hours of enjoyment should be respected without question.

"I will not tear him down further because it's more a commentary on my shortcomings than any Mr. Hemingway ever had in his life.

"And, if I'm honest, I did like The Old Man and the Sea."

Teddy closed his laptop and went to the copy center at the union. He made two copies, removed the original from the plastic report cover, and inserted the new one.

A lifetime of buried anger that stretched back to first-grade teachers and third-grade bullies floated away into the ether as Teddy walked back toward Dr. Wellington's office. Teddy eased the outer office door open and quiet as a mouse set the paper on Ruth's desk.

Teddy made his way to Hamilton Hall where Allison was taking her architectural history final. He checked his phone's clock, and it'd be as much as an hour before she would be done. He sat down on just inside the front set of doors. He texted his mom, "I'm done with my semester. It was a great semester. How's Mr. Chompers?"

"He misses you, but your father and I make sure he gets plenty of floor time. Mr. Chompers and your father have bonded."

"That's cool. I'll see you soon. Hug."

"See you Friday, Teddy bear."

Teddy looked up, and Allison was standing in front of him. Her hair was pulled back, she wore a Cincinnati Bengals sweatshirt and some black sweatpants. "How did it go?"

"I'm glad I took that break with you last night because when I got home, I did some serious book learning. I just got done kicking butt."

"You're the WoMan."

"Did you hand in your paper?"

Teddy took the copy out from his bag and flipped to the last page. He handed it to Allison.

She read it and said, "Nice quote, Monkey."

"That's Monkey King."

Allison gave him back the paper and linked her arm with his. "You know, Trish left this morning for Christmas break."

"Really?"

"I was thinking we could go back there for lunch... more of a picnic."

"A picnic sounds great."

"I've got beer, crackers, and naked, how does that sound?"

"I love you."

"I love you, too."

The End

Reach the Author

Reach the Author at:
Blog: ExtremelyAverage.com
Twitter: Twitter.com/ExtremelyAvg
Email: EcoandleRiel@gmail.com
Facebook: Facebook.com/Brian.D.Meeks

About the Author

Arthur Byrne doesn't exist except in the pages of *Underwood, Scotch, and Wry* and soon in the sequel, *Underwood, Scotch, and Cry*.

Brian D. Meeks, however, does exist.

The author can be found at his blog, http://ExtremelyAverage.com or on Twitter @ExtremelyAvg. His bio on Twitter sums him up well. " I have delusions of novelist, am obsessed with my blog, college football, and occasionally random acts of napping. I also Mock! Will follow cats & guinea pigs.

Made in the USA
Middletown, DE
03 December 2016